My Father, the Coach

OTHER BOOKS BY ALFRED SLOTE

My Father, the Coach

by Alfred Slote

*Fr Ue Family Heit
with best wishes
Alfred Slote
4/16*

J. B. LIPPINCOTT COMPANY

PHILADELPHIA AND NEW YORK

U.S. Library of Congress Cataloging in Publication Data

Slote, Alfred.
  My father, the coach.

  SUMMARY: Ezell's father finagles a Little League team for Ezell and
his friends with himself as coach, a job he's never had before.
  [1. Baseball—Stories] I. Title.
PZ7.S635My   [Fic]   72-1816
ISBN-0-397-31413-2

FOR GARNET R. GARRISON

My Father,
the Coach

ONE

THEY SAY LIGHTNING doesn't strike in the same place twice. But they say it wrong because I saw it happen.

That is one part of this story. The other parts are my pa and my best friend Obey Parker.

Obey's real name is Obadiah, though no one calls him that except his mother. And when she says "Obadiah," it sounds sweet. When we say it, Obey gets mad and his fists fly and no one in his right mind thinks calling Obey "Obadiah" is worth a bloody nose.

Obey has lived next door to us as long as I can remember. He and I used to share the same playpen. At least, that's what the old photographs say. We've been to birthday parties together as long as I can remember, and we had our share of fights and good times.

Last few years, we've had different interests, though. Back when I was nine I got a library card and started reading. Obey thinks books are for the birds and says there isn't anything you can't learn from life you can learn out of a book. He's wrong, and he should know better, because one of the first books he should have read that first season of organized ball—but he didn't—was the rule book of the Arborville Baseball Leagues. I was the only one who read the rule book, which is how I discovered the "darkness rule."

It isn't called the "darkness rule." It's just a rule in the book that says if a game has to be called before the end of the seventh inning, the score then goes back to the end of the last completed inning. We call it the "darkness rule" because it's darkness that causes most games to end early, and it was darkness that made the mess that happened to us in our first season of organized ball.

Obey is wrong about books, but he's right about everything else, especially people. Obey's got an understanding of people that's uncanny. I mean, he can tell you what a guy is like after meeting him for two seconds. That and his being the best athlete on Sumpter Street have made Obey the leader of our gang. What Obey says, we do. What Obey thinks, we think. What Obey wants, we get.

That is why it was so bad for me when Obey and my pa became enemies for a while last summer. It didn't last long, but while it did it was bad, because I thought Obey was right and my pa was wrong.

I *knew* Obey was right and my pa was wrong, and I was ashamed of my father. When you're real small you don't really think about your folks. Your pa's your pa, your ma's your ma, and you don't really see them the way other people see them. But the last few years I've been seeing my pa the way other people saw him, and I didn't like it.

For one thing, my pa's comical. He's a little guy with a high squeaky voice and a porkpie fisherman's hat, and everyone calls him "Willie." Which is his name, but it drives my mother crazy that people call Pa "Willie" who don't know him and whom he doesn't know.

Pa insists a lot of people know him that he doesn't know.

10

And he says it's OK to call him "Willie" because that is his name.

"Your name, Mr. Corkins," Ma says, grimly, "is Willard W. Corkins."

Pa grins. He says Ma doesn't understand that he is a public figure. He runs the Arborville Bank parking lot, and since the bank is in the center of town and a lot of people use the lot as a shortcut, a lot of people have come to "know" Pa. People like saying "Hello, Willie," or "How's the boy, Willie?" or "How's it going, Willie?" and Pa says "Just fine," though he doesn't know who they are and doesn't care.

That kind of thing drives my mother crazy and is one reason she hates visiting my father in the parking lot. But she has to because Pa is very absent-minded and he is always forgetting things. Usually I'm the one who gets to bring him stuff he's forgotten unless I'm in school and Pa needs it right away.

During one week I can remember bringing Pa his coffee Thermos, a Phillips head screwdriver that belonged to the bank, the big bank umbrella, his wallet, his house key. And I hated going each time, too, because like Ma I was ashamed of Pa's job in the parking lot.

I loved Pa and I know Ma loved him because when he wasn't around she always stood up for him, but he drove her crazy because he was so forgetful, because he had no ambition, because he didn't mind strangers calling him "Willie," because he always wore that porkpie hat and pushed it back on his head and scratched his forehead when he was worried, and because he always said dumb things like: "So I told that Mr. Robert Gardner just where to get off at . . ." chuckling at making himself the hero of all his stories be-

11

cause he never was the hero and he never told Mr. Robert Gardner off in all his life and never would. And he knew we knew it.

The Arborville Bank is sometimes called Gardner's Bank, because old man Gardner is president of the bank and his son Mr. Robert Gardner, who is about Pa's age, is one of the vice-presidents. I guess Mr. Robert Gardner may have been the only person in Arborville that Pa resented being called "Willie" by, but I didn't find that out till that first season of organized ball.

I found out a lot of things that first season. About Pa, about my friend Obey, about myself. And I wouldn't have found out anything if Pa hadn't finally started a baseball team on Sumpter Street.

TWO

THE ARBORVILLE KIDS' Baseball League is made up of neighborhood baseball teams. Most neighborhoods have parks big enough to include a diamond or two, but all we've got is Sumpter Street Playground with two painted, peeling teeter-totters and a concrete basketball court. And that's one reason we never had a baseball team.

I'm not knocking our old cement court, because out of it have come some of the best basketball players in Arborville. Guys like Obey's brothers Lee and Jeff, Chico's brother Tony, Spider Williams and George Copp's cousin Tom Howell. These were guys who went right from our cement court to the Arborville High varsity and played college ball, too.

On that old court, surrounded on one side by a lumber-yard and on another by a junk yard, games go on from morning to night, spring, summer, fall, and winter when the snow's been shoveled off. Big kids and little kids go to the boards together. Bloody noses, black eyes, bumps, and bruises, you just pick yourself up off the cement and go back down the court. If you don't, there's always some guy by the teeter-totter waiting to take your place.

The best of the basketball players our age—eleven—is Obey, with Tom Martin and George Copp right behind. Yet, if you were to ask Obey what his sport's going to be, he always says: "Baseball, man. What else?"

"What else?" Les Tidwell once said, "You never even played in a real baseball game so how do you know baseball's your main sport?"

"I know," Obey growled and looked so fierce Les backed off. Obey's got long arms that can flick out and grab you up tight.

Obey liked baseball so much that that is what we always talked about, even while we were clowning around on the basketball court. We played so many imaginary games that we even had everybody set in a position. The two most obvious were Gary Willets, who could throw a stone eighty miles an hour and who was always throwing things—Gary had to be our pitcher—and Obey, who had to be the catcher. Why catcher? Because, as he pointed out, he was the leader, and the catcher is the take-charge guy. He's the only one who's facing out and seeing if everyone is playing his position correctly. Catcher's the one who controls the game by controlling the pitcher. Catcher's the one who can fuss the other team by talking to the batters, by talking to the bench. Catcher's closest one to the ump so he can beef for everyone.

"Suppose you're no good, though?" Tidwell had the nerve to suggest.

Obey just looked at him. "Man," he said, "you don't want to live long, do you?"

"OK," Les said, "you got a great arm."

So Obey was set at catcher. Big George Copp had to play first since he was too slow to play anywhere else. Ed Moore swore he was a natural at third base. "I'm built like an ape," Ed said. "All the great ones were."

14

"Yeah, like Brooks Robinson," Tidwell said. "He's the only ape that looks like a string bean."

"He's an exception," Ed said. "Besides, he's over the hill, and I'm on my way up."

It didn't make any difference because no one else wanted to play third. Chico Martinez said he'd be the shortstop because he had great lateral movement.

"A basketball court ain't the same thing as a ball diamond," Tidwell objected.

"Lateral movement is lateral movement anyways you cut it," Chico snapped.

Claude Martin put in a bid for second. He was small, quick, and no one objected. Tom Martin, who is Claude's first cousin, claimed center field. "Center fielder's got to run like a deer and have a great arm, and that's me," Tom said. "You remember how I ran when the cops chased us out of the playground last Christmas."

They'd locked the playground; we'd climbed the fence and shot baskets Christmas Eve until some people living nearby objected. The police were called. We all were equal in getting back over the fence, but no one could match Tom's long strides running down Sumpter Street.

While Tidwell was worrying that one over, I said quietly that I thought I belonged in left field.

"Why left field?" Tidwell demanded.

" 'Cause that's where the power hitters play," Obey said, grinning. And everyone laughed. Tidwell and I were the poorest athletes on the street. Of course, in another neighborhood I might have been a star, but around guys like Obey, Gary, George, Ed, the Martins . . . it was just no go.

"Well, Tidwell," Obey said, "that leaves right field. How about it?"

"That's where the worst players play," Tidwell objected.

"Clemente? Frank Robinson?" Chico asked.

"OK," Les said, "I'll play there."

"While you guys were having pipe dreams, the court came free. Let's go," George said.

Baseball was just that, a pipe dream you played in the street or watched on TV. Once in a while we'd take the long walk to West Park and bang a ball around and try to work up a game, but we never had enough guys. Once in a while too we'd go there and watch the Arborville kids' baseball teams play in their jazzy white uniforms with their sponsors' names on the back, and new white balls, and umpires, and fathers pretending they were big league coaches giving all kinds of signals, and the kids screeching at each other.

We could have beat any of those teams, but we never got that chance. All we had was the lineup of a team that didn't exist.

And then one day we got our chance.

It was late May, and my pa came home from the bank around 5:30 feeling good. He kissed the twins and kissed my mother, which he only does when he feels good, and then he slapped me on the shoulder which he never did, feeling good or bad.

"*Mister* Corkins," my mother said, though she looked a little pleased to see him happy, "just what is going on?"

"Big things, woman," Pa said, and giggled. He pushed his silly porkpie hat back, sat down on a chair, and reached for a toothpick. "Big things."

My mother wiped her hands and sat down with him. I knew what she was thinking. She couldn't wait for the day when he got out of the parking lot and got an "inside" job at the bank.

16

"What kind of things, Mr. Corkins?" she asked Pa.

If he was aware of her interest, he didn't show it. He looked at me. "Ezell," he said to me, "how'd you like to play in the Arborville Baseball League this season?"

"Mr. Corkins, is that your big thing?"

"It is, woman," Pa said. "What's wrong with it?" He turned back to me. "The manager of Atlas Movers was in the lot today and he happened to mention that the moving company was looking for a kids' baseball team to sponsor, and I casually mentioned that I knew a team that wouldn't mind being sponsored. The Sumpter Street boys. Well now, what do you think of that?"

"Not much," Ma said. "I was hoping you had important news for me, Mr. Corkins."

"Why," said Pa, winking at me, "I been saving the best part till the end." Pa pulled a little blue and white book out of his pocket and tossed it on the table.

"Look at that," he said.

My mother picked it up and read out loud: "*Rules of the Arborville Recreation Baseball Leagues* . . . Mr. Corkins, what is going on?"

"That's my own personal copy, woman," Pa said, in a rather lordly tone, I thought. "Given to me by the manager of the Atlas Movers."

"And I thought you had something important to tell me."

"I do, Mrs. Corkins. I am going to coach a baseball team."

"Mr. Corkins, you're out of your mind."

Ma stood up. She was angry. I thought she was going to heave the rule book at him. Pa took it from her quickly and set it on the table. I picked it up. "Sit down, Mrs. Corkins," Pa said.

17

"I will not sit down, and you are *not* going to coach a baseball team, Mr. Corkins. You have enough to do already without taking on a baseball team. This house needs a paint job, the front steps need fixing; you promised me you were going to seal the cracks in the basement and work with me on the garden. And then, Mr. Corkins, if you have any spare time after that, I think you might find a way to improve your working conditions at the bank."

"What's wrong with my working conditions?" Pa said.

"Working all your life in a parking lot!"

"I run that lot, woman. I manage it. I direct it."

"You direct a bunch of foolish old ladies who can't drive and that gives you a feeling of accomplishing something. And now you want to manage a children's baseball team when all the while you should be trying to amount to something, Mr. Corkins."

"Woman," Pa said, and I knew he was getting mad, "you try me hard."

"Evidently not hard enough. You will not coach a baseball team."

"I will," Pa said. "I have always wanted to coach a team and I will."

"Then that is the extent of your ambition, is it? That is what you've always wanted to do."

Ma was too quick, too bright for Pa. She could twist his own words into a hard little heap and bang him over the head with it.

"Mrs. Corkins," Pa said slowly, "I will not be the only person in the Arborville Bank coaching a team. Mr. Robert Gardner coaches a team, and he is a vice-president. In fact . . ." Pa sat up straight in his chair, his eyes gleamed, "in fact, I will be coaching a team in the same eleven-year-old league his team is in. His team has won the championship the past two years. But with Ezell and Obey and George and the Martin cousins, their day is coming to an end. Yes, sir, Mr. Robert Gardner, we are going to get you. . . ."

Pa wasn't talking to us anymore. He was talking to Mr. Robert Gardner who wasn't even in the room. Ma didn't say anything. Her face had a worried expression. "Mr. Corkins," she said gently, "I am beginning to worry about you."

Pa snapped out of it. "Worry about Mr. Gardner," Pa said, with a laugh. He turned to me. "Ezell, what do you think of it?"

I put the rule book down. "It's OK," I said cautiously.

Pa looked hurt. "If you were Obey Parker, you would be jumping for joy."

"You just be glad, Mr. Corkins, you have a child like Ezell and not like Obadiah Parker, bouncing a basketball day and night like a robot. A fat lot of good that will do him. Ezell, hang up your pa's coat and call the twins to the table."

"I will hang up my own coat," Pa said, and stood up. "Ezell, we got to have a team meeting. Tomorrow night at 7:30. Can you get the boys over here?"

"I'll try."

"Do more than try, Ezell," Pa said, "you get them here."

He was trying to sound like a coach, and it almost worked, except that as he turned away from the table something in his pocket caught on a chair and came clattering down. It was a block of wood with a key attached to it. It said ARBORVILLE BANK on it; it was the key to Pa's "office."

Pa picked it up off the floor.

"Isn't that supposed to stay at the bank, Mr. Corkins?"

19

Pa laughed. "I guess I forgot to leave it there."

"Mr. Corkins, do you think you can remember enough from day to day to coach a baseball team if you can't remember to hang a simple key up inside the bank?"

"I can remember, woman," Pa said and started to leave.

"Mr. Corkins!" Ma said.

Pa turned and put up his hands just in time. The blue and white rule book came flying through the air. Pa caught it.

"I don't care for baseball rule books on my dinner table," Ma said coldly. "Please call the twins."

Pa glared at her, stuck the rule book back in his pocket, and left. When he'd gone, some of the starchiness went out of my mother. She slumped a little and looked at me. "What am I going to do?"

"What's wrong?"

"Your pa a baseball coach. Ezell, if nothing else is wrong, your pa doesn't know anything about baseball."

"He can learn."

"At his age? And will your friends let him? Do you really think boys like Obey Parker and George Copp and Ed Moore are going to let Willard W. Corkins coach them in baseball?"

I didn't know. The way she said it, I kind of doubted it. Although they wouldn't say anything to me, I knew my friends thought of my father as a kind of comical figure. I did too, sometimes.

"Ezell," Ma said softly, "if he insists on coaching, they got to let him."

I stared at her. "Ma, first you say he shouldn't coach a team, then you say they got to want him as coach."

"They got to, Ezell. This is more than baseball to your father. He's doing this because of that Mr. Robert Gardner."

"Well, if Obey comes on the team, the other guys will, too. And when that happens, we'll blow Mr. Gardner and his Arborville Bank team right out of sight, Ma."

"That's exactly what I'm worried about," Ma said. "Then your father *will* be stuck in that bank parking lot the rest of his life."

For Pete's sake, I thought. What did she want?

Since I didn't know, I decided my best policy would be to keep my mouth shut. And I did.

THREE

OBEY WAS THE key man. If Obey came on the team, so would the other guys. The next morning I went over to Obey's house at 7:45. Mrs. Parker, a little surprised, let me in.

"Aren't you a little early, Ezell?"

"Yes, ma'am. I thought I'd get a jump on school."

She smiled. Anything that had to do with school and books, Mrs. Parker approved of. She liked me because she thought I'd be a good influence on Obey, get his mind off ball and onto books. Though it usually worked the other way around. He got my mind off books and onto ball.

"Well, I just wish Obadiah felt like getting a jump on school sometimes. He'll probably jump when it's too late. Obadiah," she called.

Obey came out of the kitchen with crumbs on his mouth. He looked half-asleep. His theory about school was that if you slept late enough you might not have to go.

"You're early," he grunted at me.

"I got important stuff to talk about."

"Yeah? What?"

"Get your books, I'll tell you on the way."

22

"I got no books. Let's go now."

"Hold on now," Mrs. Parker said and gave Obey a grim look. "How come you got no books to take and Ezell is carrying two books?"

Obey gave me one of his now-look-what-you've-done-to-me-Ezell looks.

"Ma," he said, "Ezell is always carrying books. He does that real good . . ."

Obey ducked as Mrs. Parker's right hand reached out for him. Then he grabbed his jacket off a doorknob and was out the front door, all in one easy fluid motion. What an athlete!

Mrs. Parker was not admiring him, however. "Someday that child will learn not to smart-lip people. Ezell, you will be doing Obadiah a great favor if you encourage him to read a book sometime. He has a lot of friends who encourage him to play ball and not a one except you who could encourage him to read."

I didn't know what to say to that. The reason I'd come over early was to talk Obey into coming onto my father's new baseball team. But I wasn't going to tell Mrs. Parker that.

"You still go to the library every Friday, don't you, Ezell?"

"Yes, ma'am."

"Take Obadiah with you sometime."

"Yes, ma'am. I'll try."

She smiled at my "I'll try." Then she said: "You better run along now before you're late. I don't think that rascal child of mine has even waited for you."

But she was wrong. Obey was waiting for me at the corner and when I came up he gave me his suspicious look. "What was you and she talking about, Ezell?"

23

"You."

"What did she wanna know?"

"If I'd take you to the library some Friday."

"That all?"

"Yeah."

He was relieved. "I thought it was something serious. She keeps bugging me about reading books. Hey, what've you got on your mind so important?"

I took a deep breath. Here we go, I thought.

"My pa's starting a baseball team."

"You jokin'?"

"No. They asked my pa if he'd coach a ball team in the eleven-year-old league, sponsored by the Atlas Movers. He said yes."

"A team from around here?"

"Yes. You, Tom, Claude, George, Ed, Gary, Chico, Les . . . all the guys."

"Hot damn!" Obey banged his fist into his palm. "That just ain't bad at all, is it? We finally get into organized ball. Who you asked so far, Ezell?"

"Just you."

"I'll get the others, don't you worry about that." Obey chuckled. "I'll put big George on first, Claude at second, Ed at third, I'll put Chico—" He stopped himself as though he was hearing his words for the first time.

"Ezell," he said.

"What?"

"Your pa can't coach."

"Sure he can," I said weakly.

I guess I'd known from the beginning this was going to happen.

"Uh-uh, no way. He's not the coach type. Don't get mad

24

now, 'cause it's true. I like your pa a lot, but he can't coach a ball team. He don't even throw right, Ezell."

Obey meant that when my pa threw a ball it was like a girl throws, all elbow and wrist.

"You don't have to throw to coach," I said, which was entirely reasonable and all wrong, as I knew.

"Ezell," Obey said, and patted me on the shoulder, "don't you worry. I'm gonna figure this out. We can't pass up this chance to have a real team. But your pa . . . he's got to let me do the coaching."

"I don't know about that, Obey."

"You want to have a ball team or not, Ezell?"

"But—"

"Ain't no buts, man. Everything in life's got a condition. Look, there's Claude and Tom. I'll ask them and you see what they say."

There was no arguing with Obey and part of me knew he was right. My pa wasn't the coach type. He didn't look like a coach, sound like a coach, smell like a coach. You looked at my pa and smiled and said: "How're things in the parking lot, Willie?" That wasn't how you talked to a coach.

Claude and Tom Martin were waiting for us on the corner of Fourth and Detroit. They were first cousins but very different. Tom was tall and thin, a great athlete but also a great worrier. Claude was short and stocky and intelligent. He was always a heads-up ball player.

"You guys hear the news?" Obey asked, as we came up to them. I liked Obey's approach to things. It was direct, to say the least.

"What news?" Tom asked, suspiciously.

"New baseball team's being formed."

"Which league?" Claude asked, under the impression it was either the American or National League.

25

Obey laughed. "I ain't talking about the major leagues, Claude man. I'm talking about the Arborville Kids' Baseball League. The eleven-year-old league, as a matter of fact."

"Yeah? So what's that got to do with us?" Tom asked.

"What's it got to do with us?" Obey repeated and slapped Tom on the back, moving him about three feet forward on the sidewalk. "It's got everything to do with us, man. Me and Ezell are forming this team."

"Funny," Claude said. "We already got a team that doesn't play games."

Obey laughed. "Well, this team's already been accepted into the Arborville Baseball League. How do you like that?"

"Accepted by who?" Tom asked.

"By who? By whoever does the accepting," Obey said, beginning to get irritated. "How do I know?"

Both Martins looked at each other. They were beginning to realize that Obey wasn't kidding.

"You mean," Claude said slowly, still not daring to really believe it—we'd talked so long about being a real team and playing real games with umpires and bases that neither he nor Tom could really believe it was going to come true— "you mean, a real team with *uniforms?*"

"Sure, with uniforms," Obey said impatiently. "What kind of a team plays without uniforms? And new balls and new bats too."

"Who's paying for this?" Tom asked suspiciously.

Obey sighed. "The Atlas Movers, that's who."

"Who're they?"

"Only the biggest moving company in town, that's all."

"How come they want *us* on their team?"

"Tom, you just won't believe a thing, will you? Well, I

26

just told you. They don't want us on their team. They ain't even got a team. They want us to *be* their team."

"I'm still asking: how come us?"

Obey looked as though he were going to pop Tom one, he was so exasperated. Then he shrugged. "You tell them, Ezell."

The Martins looked at me.

"It's true," I said. "The Atlas Movers want to enter a team in the eleven-year-old league and my pa said he'd coach one from this neighborhood."

"Your pa?" Tom said.

"That's right," I said uneasily, "my pa."

The Martins looked at each other. I could see two things going through their heads. One, that it wasn't a joke; it was true. Two, that it could be a joke if it was true, 'cause of my pa.

Claude turned to me. "No disrespect, Ezell, but your pa's no coach."

"We got that all settled already," Obey said quickly.

"How you got it settled?"

"I'm gonna do the coaching."

"Oh."

"What about Ezell's pa?" Claude asked.

"He's gonna manage, like," Obey said. "Be the head man. Paper work, handle money, stuff like that."

"Suppose he wants to be the field coach," Tom asked, "then what?"

"Then," Obey acknowledged, "we got problems."

"Maybe," Claude said, working it out in his head, "Obey could be the coach without your pa knowing it, Ezell."

"Now how is that gonna happen?" Tom demanded.

"Heck, I don't know how. Maybe we call Ezell's pa 'Coach' but we do what Obey tells us to do. No disrespect

27

meant, Ezell, but your pa don't even throw a ball right."

"Forget it," Obey said quickly. "Ezell don't mind if his father don't coach, and probably Mr. Corkins won't mind either—"

"If we win," Tom said.

"Well, what do you think we're gonna do? Lose?" Obey slammed his fist into his palm. "Man," he said softly, "I been waiting all my life for this day. A real ball team. The Atlas Movers. That's a great name. We're gonna move those other teams right out of there. We're gonna hit those guys like they never been hit before. Hey, let's hustle to school. I got to get hold of Gary, Ed, George, Chico, Tidwell. We got to have a team meeting right away."

"Tonight at my house at 7:30. My pa wants us to meet," I said.

Claude and Tom looked at Obey questioningly. Suppose Obey didn't want to have a meeting tonight at 7:30 at Ezell Corkins's house?

But Obey just grinned. "No problem. Ezell's pa coaches off the field. I coach on the field. Atlas Movers, here we come. Let's go—"

And Obey took off like a streak, knees pumping high down Miller Avenue toward school. Tom and Claude yelled and took off right behind him. I hesitated. I felt I had just betrayed Pa, but what else could I have done?

I took off right behind them.

FOUR

BY SEVEN THIRTY, our little living room was crammed with the guys, plus my twin sisters Marie and Louisa who kept running in and out, shrieking and giggling and pretending we were tripping them. Finally my mother made them go upstairs to their room.

All the guys except for Obey sat on the floor. Obey sat in a chair waiting for my father to get the meeting started. Pa sat in his favorite chair in the corner, wearing his porkpie hat, and he had papers spread out on his lap. He kept shuffling the papers. I knew he wanted to start off with a strong pep talk, but now that the guys were actually there, looking at him, waiting, he'd forgot what he wanted to say. So he fiddled with his papers until finally I said: "Pa, everyone's here."

"Well, so they are. Yes, indeed, they are. I guess I'll count you boys. Let's see, Ezell, there's Obey, Tom Martin, Claude Martin, Gary Willets, George Copp—hello, George."

"Hello, Mr. Corkins."

"How's your father, George?"

"He's fine, Mr. Corkins."

"You say hello to him for me, will you now?"

"Yes, sir."

Tom and Claude looked at each other and then at Obey, but Obey wouldn't look their way. He kept his eyes glued on my father, who finally got through his private conversation with George. Pa was just a friendly person and that was the long and short of it.

"Let's see, and there's Chico, Ed Moore. How's your pa, Ed?"

"OK," Ed said.

"You say hello to him for me. And Lester Tidwell. How are you, Mr. Tidwell?"

"Fine, Mr. Corkins," Les said, and we all laughed.

Tidwell was the team comedian. Even when he didn't say funny things they seemed funny.

"Well now," Pa went on, pushing his porkpie back on his head, "that makes nine of you and nine is what you need for a baseball team, as I remember the rules of the game."

He was making a joke. I hoped someone would laugh, but no one did.

Obey cut in. "We'll need more than nine guys, Mr. Corkins. We'll need at least one substitute if someone gets hurt."

"Or goes on vacation," Tom said.

"Who is gonna go on vacation during baseball season, Tom?" Obey asked.

No one answered. And then Tidwell, who hadn't any sense and never went on vacation anytime anywhere, spoke up.

"I might," Les said.

And that started laughter.

"Knock it off," Obey growled. "Tidwell, if you want to play on this team, keep the funny lines down. We're here to get a ball club going, not a comedy act."

Pa's eyebrows shot up. I knew he didn't know what to say. Tom and Claude looked at each other again.

Obey turned to my pa. "Mr. Corkins, what do the rules say about playing with eight guys if someone gets hurt?"

"The rules?" Pa repeated. "That's right. I got a rule book right here. Let's see, where did I leave it? Ezell, have you seen the rule book? It's got a blue and white cover."

"I saw it last night, Pa, but you took it back."

"Mr. Corkins," my mother said from the other room, "I remember your taking it to the bank this morning. You said you were going to study it in your free moments."

"Why . . . so I did," Pa said, and scratched his forehead. He looked around at us and smiled. "And that is what I did."

"You undoubtedly have forgot again and left it there," Ma said.

"Well, now that you mention it, I guess that is what I did," Pa said, and laughed. "No harm done. I'll get it in the morning. No one is going to steal a copy of the Arborville baseball rules out of the bank. Ezell and I are going to study that book, boys, and we'll let you know what it says about playing with eight players. Now . . . let's see, item number two—money. Yes, sir, money. It says here that each boy playing in the league has got to pay a dollar as dues."

"What for?" Chico asked.

"To pay the umps," Obey said, "buy new bases. Stuff like that."

"Exactly right," Pa said.

How Obey knew these things I didn't know. I guess guys who are going to make sports their life career just find out everything ahead of time.

"I don't have a dollar," Tidwell said.

"If anyone can't get themselves a dollar, I'll lend them one," Pa said.

"*Well* now," my ma said from the other room. I wondered if she was sitting by the door listening.

"Tidwell, you got money," Obey said.

"No, I don't, Obey."

"Yes, you do," Obey growled. Tidwell shrugged. "OK, so I got money," he said.

Pa beamed. "All right, boys. Now along with the dollar I got to get your folks' permission for you to play. They got to sign up on these little white cards. Ezell, will you pass these around?"

He handed me a stack of cards to pass out. They said ARBORVILLE RECREATION BASEBALL LEAGUES on top.

"Can I get an uncle to sign for me?" Tidwell asked, embarrassed.

Tidwell had a lot of uncles but no pa.

"If any of them can write," Chico said, with a grin.

Tidwell got mad. "Listen, smart alec. You wanna fight—"

"Shut up," Obey said. "Anyone can sign it. I'll sign it for you. They don't even look at those cards."

"Now, how do you know that, Obey?" George Copp asked. George was maybe the only guy on the team not physically afraid of Obey. He was bigger than Obey. Slower, too, though, and because he was slower Obey was able to beat him in wrestling. In just about any sport. But just the same, George wasn't afraid of Obey, and Obey knew it.

"My pa coached my brother Lee's team years ago."

"Hey, what about your pa coaching—" Tidwell started,

and then suddenly stopped as Obey hit him with a hard look.

"Good," Pa said, checking off that item on his lap. "We got that settled. Now you return those cards to me or Ezell as soon as you can. Item number three, the season starts June tenth and that is only a few weeks from now. So we got to have some practices and work hard, because, boys, I put us in the American Division of the league, which is the tough division this year."

"How come?" Tidwell asked.

" 'Cause that's where we belong," Obey said. "You did exactly right, Mr. Corkins."

"Thank you, Obey. Let me explain about these here two divisions. After last year's season, they took the top four teams in each division and lumped them into one division and the bottom eight in the other. That way the games would be closer. I got us into the top division."

"I still wanna know why," Tidwell said.

Pa leaned forward. "Because, Mr. Tidwell, that is where the Arborville Bank team is. They was last year's champs. They's a team that hasn't lost a game in two years. And they is just sitting up there cocky and smart and rich waiting for you boys from Sumpter Street who are gonna knock them off their fat perches."

"Say, Mr. Corkins, isn't that the bank you work for?" Chico was absolutely incredulous.

"That's right," Pa said, grinning.

The guys looked at each other, a little bewildered—like they thought my pa was crazy. Pa laughed. "Anyways, you get the most out of beating the best, isn't that right, Obey?"

"You bet that's right, Mr. Corkins," Obey said.

"OK," Tidwell said, "but if we're gonna beat that bank

team, Mr. Corkins, you got to let me pitch. Willets here thinks he's our pitcher, but I got a curve ball that'll give those rich kids hernias."

Everyone laughed except Gary Willets, who never liked jokes about pitchers or pitching.

"Tidwell," Gary said slowly, "you can barely throw a ball across this room."

"Tidwell," Chico said, "if you pitch I'm bettin' on the other team."

"Tidwell," Tom said, "if you pitch, it means no one else showed up."

Claude turned to Obey. "You're not gonna let Tidwell pitch, are you?"

Obey grinned and shook his head. "Tidwell's in right field where he always was."

"I got short," Chico said.

"Third," Ed said.

"Second," Claude put in.

"Center," Tom said.

"I'm at first," George said in his deep bass.

"And I'm pitching," Gary said, curling his big hand around an imaginary ball, "and when I'm foggin' them through, it won't matter where you guys play. I'm gonna strike 'em all out."

Pa laughed—his happy high squeaky laugh. I guess he didn't mind that the team was somehow all set without him having anything to do about setting it. Maybe it would all work out. Maybe Obey could coach and Pa could do the paper work and it would be OK. I didn't believe it yet, but the way Pa sat there letting us take over . . . I didn't know whether to feel good or bad, so I felt both. Bad for him, good for us.

34

"The big thing is we got to have practices," Obey said. "Mr. Corkins, you got to start reserving us the big diamond at West Park every day after school."

"Every day?" Pa said.

"Sure," Obey said. "We're two years behind those other teams."

"I won't be able to make it down there every day, Obey," Pa said apologetically.

"That's OK," Obey said. "I'll run the team when you're not there."

The rest of the guys nodded. I knew then they were wise to what was happening.

"How do I reserve the diamond, Obey?" Pa asked, a little doubtful.

"You call the Recreation Department at Thompson School. Tell them you want Diamond Number One, that's the big diamond, at West Park every day from 4:00 to 6:00 P.M."

"Obey, I got a paper route," Ed Moore said.

"Get your kid brother to take it over," Obey said.

"Where we gonna get balls and bats?"

"At the equipment room at Thompson School. Mr. Corkins'll call and tell them we don't have anything."

"Do we get new bats and new balls, Obey?"

"You're *darn* right we do," Obey said, "but we got to save the new balls for games. I'll go down with you to pick out bats, Mr. Corkins."

"How are we gonna get to West Park, anyway?"

"On legs, Chico," Obey snapped.

"Some of the games are gonna be way out at Buhr and Vets and Sampson," George Copp said. "How we gonna get there, Obey?"

35

"Mr. Corkins'll arrange that."

"That's right," Pa said, a little awed, I thought, at Obey's decisiveness.

"Are we gonna have Atlas Movers on our shirts, Obey?"

"What do you think we're gonna have, Tidwell? Toledo Mudhens?"

"How about baseball shoes?"

"You got to get your own. All they'll give us is cap, shirt, pants, and socks. You got to get your own shoes."

"What do shoes cost?"

"Plenty."

"Tidwell can play in sneakers."

"I'll get shoes," Tidwell said defiantly, and Obey laughed.

"OK," Obey said, and his eyes were shining as he turned to Pa. There was no doubt in anyone's mind now as to who was running the ball club. My pa had just let Obey Parker take over right in front of everyone. I hoped Obey wouldn't push it too far. He didn't.

"The big thing now, Coach, is you got to line us up some practice games. You got to call up the other coaches and book games with them."

It was the first time tonight anyone had called my father "Coach," and it had come from the most important guy on the team. Pa couldn't help smiling.

"I will, Obey. I got a list of the other coaches and I'll start calling them tomorrow."

Obey nodded approvingly.

FIVE

IT WAS REALLY kind of wonderful to see Pa so happy. After the guys had left, he came back in the living room, rubbing his hands together and saying: "A real baseball team, that's what we got, Mrs. Corkins. A real ball club."

"Hadn't you better wait till you see them play, Mr. Corkins?" Ma asked sensibly.

Pa laughed. "Woman, I don't have to see them play. I can smell athletes when I'm around them. Those boys are good. And that Obey, he's a real take-charge type, isn't he?"

I looked at Pa to see if he was kidding, but he wasn't. I knew then that he was grateful that Obey was taking charge. Pa didn't really want to coach baseball; he just wanted a baseball team of his own to beat the bank team to death with.

"Ezell, you think I ought to make up a lineup or should I let Obey do it?"

I was tempted to say: "You do it, Pa," but I didn't.

"Obey knows the guys, Pa, why don't you let him do it?"

"I will. But you know what I can do now? I can find out when we can get our equipment, because we're surely not

37

going to be able to hold any practices without bats and balls, now, are we?"

Pa clapped his hands, as if he were a football player breaking from a huddle. "I'm going to call Mr. Domres right now. He's president of the league and a big lawyer in town. Yes, sir, I'll call Tom Domres right now."

Pa liked saying "Tom Domres" so much he repeated it twice more, on the way to the phone. Ma sighed. She was strengthening buttons on the twins' spring coats. She looked over at me.

"You think it went all right, Ezell?"

"Yeah."

"You don't think he minds Obey Parker coaching his team, do you?"

"Nope. Do you?"

"No," she said, and smiled sadly, "though part of me wishes he did."

"Me too."

"Well, we better let well enough alone."

"I know, Ma, but it makes me feel bad."

"I know how you feel, Ezell. But believe me, it will all work out for the best this way. Obey Parker is a remarkable boy. If I never believed it before, I believed it tonight, listening to him handle everyone and then calling your pa 'Coach.' I just hope Obey continues to stay on your pa's good side."

"And the other way around, too, 'cause—"

"Shsh."

Pa came back in the room, pushed his porkpie back on his head, and scratched his forehead. It was his move when he was vaguely dissatisfied with something.

"Well, I found we can't get any equipment till Friday night. When the season starts, the equipment room at

38

Thompson School is open Monday and Wednesday nights, but now it's only every Friday night at eight o'clock. We'll just have to wait till Saturday morning for our first practice."

"Mr. Corkins, may I remind you that Saturday morning was the morning you promised me you were going to dig up my vegetable garden."

"That's right," Pa said, and scratched his head, "I did say that. Well, I'll just do it in the afternoon. It won't take me more than a couple of hours. Ezell, you remind me tomorrow morning to call the Recreation Department and reserve the diamond for Saturday morning. I wonder if you can reserve diamonds for Saturdays. Hmmm. You know, there's a lot more to coaching than meets the eye. And I haven't even really started coaching on the field yet."

Ma and I must have looked pretty alarmed at that because Pa laughed. "Now, don't you two worry, I won't make a fool of myself. Not flat out, anyways. By gum, if we only had that rule book to study tonight. Ezell, remind me to bring it back from the bank tomorrow, will you?"

Next morning going to school Obey showed me the lineup he'd made out the night before. He had Chico at short leading off, Claude at second batting number two, himself catching and hitting third, George at first batting fourth, Tom in center batting fifth, Ed at third batting sixth, Gary pitching and batting seventh, me in left and batting eighth, and Tidwell in right field and hitting last.

"How's she look to you?"

"OK."

"I figure Tom to be our number two pitcher, and Ed can throw 'em over the plate if he has to. Say, we gonna get the equipment today?"

39

"Nope. Not till Friday."

"Friday? You're kidding."

I explained to Obey the problem with the equipment room at Thompson School.

"Man, that means we can't have our first practice till Saturday."

"Obey, we waited two years to have a real team; we can wait a couple more days."

Obey laughed. "You're right as usual, Ezell. I'm going down with you Friday night to pick equipment though."

"I never expected anything else."

Our new team was the talk of the school all that day, but I let it float over my head. I'd had enough of baseball with the guys and at home, and now it had followed us to school. We were supposed to be doing a unit on ecology but Obey was busy telling Janet Sanders behind me about the team and Tidwell was telling some other kid about the team and I could hardly hear Mrs. Hadley talk about how sewers flowed into rivers and how rivers flowed into oceans and how everything was going to pieces.

Part of the problem was the end of school coming up in a couple of weeks. This time of year, spring, with kites flying outside, and puddles, and the sun bright and warm, it was hard to sit in school. It was hard for guys like Obey and Tidwell to sit in school anytime, but it wasn't for me. I liked school. I wouldn't admit that to anyone, even my mother (who knew anyway), but I liked reading and studying and setting down on paper what I read and what I thought of it. Summers were fine and lazy and I liked ball and fishing, but I liked school and I missed it. I was always glad when summer was over and we went back to school. But like I said, it's hard to admit things like this to people. Especially to guys you play ball with.

The guys were playing basketball after school that afternoon, but I told them I had chores to do around the house. I didn't really, but I'd had enough of them for a while. I wanted to be alone. I still had one of my library books to finish—about an Apache Indian boy named Laughing Face who was having a hard time in his tribe because he didn't have a father. Some young brave adopted him but he wasn't around to protect Laughing Face when the other Indian kids teased him. It seemed like a pretty poor thing to me, and I thought of Tidwell on our team who had no pa. No one teased Les. It didn't look like such a hot deal, being an Indian boy, but what I liked was the outdoors. They were always hunting and fishing and studying the weather and reading the outdoors like it was a book. Which I guess I'd do too if I didn't read books so much.

I stayed in my room all afternoon reading about Laughing Face, and would have read till supper if Pa hadn't come into my room.

"I brought the rule book home, Ezell. You go over it and we'll talk about it later."

He tossed it to me. Pa wasn't much of a reader, but I knew he'd ask me every question under the sun so I better read it all.

Till supper time I read that old rule book, and it wasn't half as good as Laughing Face's problems. The plot was terrible, and there were no people in it. Just a lot of things like: in the eleven-year-old league all games are seven innings long. A game is official after four complete innings. If a game is called after that but before the seventh inning, then

41

the score goes back to the score of the last completed inning. Only they didn't say "goes back," but "reverts" which I had to look up. It's bad enough looking up words in stories you like, but to go to look them up in a rule book, of all things, is a pain. Anyway, that rule was what we later came to call "the darkness rule." It would turn out to be important, but I didn't know it then.

I discovered no pitcher could pitch more than seven innings in two consecutive games; no games could be protested. Only the coach and captain could call time or speak to the umpires. And on it went, page after page of dreary rules.

I was glad when supper time came.

Pa had the sense to wait till after supper to grill me on the rules. He had the idea that Ma didn't want any baseball talk at the dinner table. The twins took over the conversation and shrieked on about some boy pulling Louisa's hair in school and how Marie kicked him in the shins for doing it. The kid had to go to the school nurse, and I thought that any kid who tangled with my little sisters deserved a medal and then a hospital bed, in that order.

After dinner Pa asked me a lot of questions and kept nodding and repeating my answers. He'd remember them for one day, maybe two, and then he'd forget. He was eager now to learn it all.

"Obey can run the team on the field," he said, "but when there's an argument about something, they'll call on me. Don't you think so, Ezell?"

"I do, Pa."

"That's why I got to know the rules. So read me that part about what a balk is when there's a runner on first . . ."

The next day the guys kept telling Obey the kind of bats they wanted him to pick out. They gave him so many suggestions that Obey made them shut up. Then he told them they could come down with him and my father when we went over to Thompson School tomorrow night.

"You think that's such a good idea?" I asked Obey as we walked home from school.

"Sure. Is there any rule in that book against it?"

"Nope, but it may be pretty hairy, nine guys running around an equipment room picking out bats."

"We'll see what happens," Obey said. "If they step out of line, I'll hammer them right back in."

Good old Obey. First he was our coach, and now he was the team cop. Maybe it was the same job.

And then finally it was Friday. For Obey and the guys it meant a trip to the equipment room in the evening. For me, it meant going to the library after school that afternoon. I still hadn't finished Laughing Face, but I could keep it another two weeks. I had two other books to return, and when I got home from school, I grabbed them and started to leave. Ma nabbed me as I hit the front porch.

"Where're you going, Ezell?"

"Aw, Ma."

"Come back in. I got something for you to deliver to your father."

"Ma, can't I ever do something without doing something else?"

That may not make any sense to you, but it did to me. If I said I was going down to the corner to see the guys, Ma would say: "On your way tell Marie and Louisa to come home." If I said I was going over to Chico's house, Ma

43

would say: "Stop at Demos's on your way back and buy me some margarine." It's like she didn't have any errands to do unless I was already going somewhere else.

This time I knew what it was the minute I saw the brown paper bag. It was my father's big Thermos inside. Pa had two coffee Thermoses, a big one and a little one. The little one he used every day of the week except Friday, when the bank stayed open till 6:00 P.M. Today, he'd taken the little one and left the big one home by mistake. So I had to take him some more hot coffee. They didn't like him coming inside the bank to drink coffee.

"It just takes a second, Ezell, and it's on your way."

"Everything's always on my way," I grumbled, but I took the bag and my books and left. The playground was on the way, and sure enough there were the Atlas Movers playing basketball.

"Hey, Ezell," Chico shouted, "we need you."

"I can't," I shouted back.

"Hey, man, it's Friday," I heard Ed Moore say. "He goes to the library on Friday."

Obey gave me a quick wave while running up the court. He took a rebound away from George Copp, whirled, and fired down court to Tom who grabbed it and put it up and in over an outstretched hand.

If the Atlas Movers were half as good at baseball as they were at basketball, we'd beat the bank team without trying.

I walked up Fifth Street, past Demos's grocery store, past the Beer Vault and the Thrift Shop, then past a whole bunch of stores, and finally onto Liberty Avenue. I turned left on Liberty and ahead of me was the Arborville Bank and Pa's parking lot.

It didn't look as crowded as it usually did on Friday, which was a big banking day. A big Cadillac was pulled up

44

alongside Pa's "office." It was nothing but a small wooden hut with a heater in it and a place for Pa to sit and write down license plates. If someone's car stayed in the lot too long, it meant he was shopping somewhere else, having gone out the front door of the bank. Pa was supposed to warn them politely, and if they did it again, he was supposed to warn them again politely.

Standing next to the big Cadillac was Pa, and he was talking to a tall dark-haired man. The guy had a set of car keys in his hand. I came up behind them, but I knew Pa had seen me. He's got great peripheral vision, Pa has.

"Come here, Ezell," Pa said, and put an arm around my shoulders. "This is my oldest child, Ezell Corkins. Ezell, this is Mr. Robert Gardner who is coach of the champeen bank team."

Pa giggled as he said "champeen," and Mr. Gardner smiled faintly. He was a big man with sideburns coming down on top of his ears. He smelled a little of after-shave lotion. I decided I didn't like him at all.

"How're you doin', Ezell?" he asked me, and gave me a wink as though he and I were in cahoots against my pa.

I didn't answer him. I turned to Pa. "I got your big Thermos," I said.

"Why, thank you, son. Stick around, now. I was just telling Mr. Gardner about our team. He's heard about us already. Yes, sir, ain't that right?"

"Nothing but bad things, Willie," Gardner said, giving me another wink. "Where do you play, Ezell?"

As far from you as possible, I thought.

"Ezell's my starting left fielder," Pa put in quickly.

I had to smile at that. With only nine guys, we all were starters.

"Good for him," Gardner said.

"Yes, sir. I got Mr. Tom Martin in center and Mr. Les Tidwell in right. Martin is faster than Bob Hayes was at his age. I got me some fleet-footed ball players on the Atlas Movers."

Mr. Robert Gardner laughed. "It's not a track meet, Willie," he said, and winked again. I guess he wasn't winking at me. It was just a nervous twitch. I still didn't like him.

"Willie, I'm gonna be leaving around five, so keep it close."

And then he flipped the car keys through the air at Pa who must have been expecting them because he caught them easily and said: "Yes, sir, I'll put it right by the back door."

"Take care, Ezell," Gardner said, and strode over to the bank and went in the back door.

"How come he doesn't park his own car?"

" 'Cause he's vice-president of the bank. That's how come."

"You don't park cars for anyone else, though."

Pa looked at me and smiled. "Ezell, there's some things you're gonna have to understand when you grow up. Like this parking lot, for instance. It's his lot. So he tells me what to do on it. He wins the battle of the parking lot, Ezell, but we are gonna get even on the ball diamond."

"Pa, here's your Thermos . . ."

"He don't own the diamond."

"Pa," I almost yelled, "here's your Thermos."

"Huh?" Pa looked down at me as though he'd forgot I was there. "Well, so it is. I didn't even remember that I forgot it. Go put it in my office while I park Coach Gardner's car. Then we'll talk over some strategy."

"Pa, I'm going to the library. Today's Friday."

"Well, so it is. I forgot that too. You run along then,

Ezell, and get out your books. It's good you like to read, son. I never did, and look where I ended up."

"Aw, Pa, don't talk like that."

Pa smiled at me. "It's OK, Ezell. We'll get us some equipment tonight and tomorrow we'll have our first practice, and when the season starts, we'll show them who we are. That is what we'll do. Yes, sir, we'll show them who we are."

Pa got into Mr. Gardner's car and drove it to a parking place not thirty feet from where we were standing.

I put the Thermos in the "office" and fled to the library.

SIX

THAT NIGHT WE SCORED our first "first" in Arborville base-ball history. Into the long narrow equipment room at Thompson School piled nine guys and their coach, and it was absolute chaos.

An older kid at the door tried to stop us, but Tidwell went under him, Chico went around him, Obey went through him, and the rest of us went over him.

"Hey, look at all these uniforms."

"There must be a thousand pairs of socks here."

"Bats, balls."

"Obey, there's the catchers' masks and shin pads."

"Hey, look at these bases stacked up here. Do we get bases?"

"No, the umps bring bases to the games."

"Caps. There're the caps. Gimme a boost up, George. What color are our caps gonna be, Mr. Corkins?"

"Hey, you kids," the kid who worked there said, having picked himself up off the floor, "get down from there. Who's the coach? Doesn't this team have a coach?"

"Cool it, fella," Chico said, "or we'll expel you from your job."

Pa tried to get the guys to put things back, settle down, but he couldn't get anyone's attention. Obey was the only one who could do that and Obey was trying on shin pads and masks. Obey was going as wild as any of them. It was a fairyland for the guys who'd never had a uniform, never had any real baseball equipment before.

"I'm gonna call Mr. Domres," the big kid wailed.

"Now, boys," Pa said, but you couldn't hear him over the din. Then into the room came a man who turned out to be Mr. Domres himself. Pa saw him right away, and embarrassed as anything, he went up to him and introduced himself. They shook hands. Mr. Domres took one look around and then started laughing.

I guess by then it was funny. Guys were trying on caps, shirts, socks, over their regular clothes. They were taking different poses, saying things like: "Take my picture, darling. I'm beautiful."

Tidwell had on a yellow and green softball shirt and a red cap, and he was trying to get room enough to swing a bat. I guess that made Mr. Domres take action. Someone could get hurt. Tidwell couldn't hit a ball but he could certainly hit George Copp, who was wearing an umpire's chest protector and an orange cap.

Mr. Domres stuck two fingers in his mouth and blew. The whistle turned us all around, and brought on silence.

"OK, men," he said with a smile, "let's get the stuff back on the shelves and pick out what belongs to you. I'm Tom Domres, president of the league. The sooner you get the stuff back, the sooner you get your own stuff."

Magic words. In a few seconds everything was back on the shelves. Not exactly the way it had been, but almost good enough. Then Mr. Domres dragged out a big equipment bag and turned it over to Pa, who turned it over to

49

Obey. Obey emptied it out on the concrete floor. There were old bats in it, old brown balls in a ball bag, catcher's equipment: mask, shin guards, a chest protector. There were batting helmets and base-running helmets and a couple of old score sheets.

Mr. Domres told us it had belonged to a ten-year-old team last year that had busted up.

"How'd they do last year?" Claude asked.

Mr. Domres looked surprised. "I don't rightly know. I'd guess they didn't do too well or they wouldn't have busted up."

"Let's get the bag of a team that didn't bust up," Tidwell said.

Mr. Domres laughed. "If you can play ball, the bag won't hurt you."

"Don't we get new bats and balls?" Obey asked.

"Yes, you do. You get six new balls and six new bats. John, bring over the boxes of balls."

The kid we'd trampled on brought over a box of baseballs. He didn't even look at us as he came over. Obey took out six balls, one at a time, and examined each one carefully, and then he tossed them into the small ball bag that went inside the big equipment bag.

"The bats are in those baskets there," Mr. Domres said.

It was the wrong thing to say, because everyone thought he meant each guy could pick his own bat, and chaos started up again. Pa tried to stop the rush to the bat baskets but everyone went around him. Then Obey went into action. He picked up Tidwell and threw him backwards. Then he grabbed Chico by the waist and tossed him the other way. He pushed Tom to one side and put a bear hug on Ed Moore and hauled him out of there. Then he had a

50

moment of truth with big George Copp who had a bat out and was starting to swing it.

"Put it down," Obey said.

"Put what down, man?"

"That bat."

"What for?"

"I'm picking the bats for the team."

"Who says so?" George kept swinging the bat. It was like he was trying it for heft and size, but the warning was there. He could as easily bring it down on Obey's head as put it back.

"I say so. I'm the captain. I can't have everyone picking out a favorite bat. We're only allowed six bats, so I'm picking them out as captain."

"Who made you captain, Obey?"

"Mr. Corkins. Ain't that right, Mr. Corkins?"

"Right," Pa said quietly. "You're captain, Obey."

"Captain picks out the bats," Obey said, as though it had been written in the Bible. I had to admire old Obey.

"Captain gonna pick out bats that suit him or that suit the team?"

"Captain is captain of the whole team, Copp. Whole team, man."

George thought it over. Then he shrugged. "This one feels good to me, Obey."

"Put it back in the basket, man." Obey was tough.

George took one last little swing and then put it back in the basket. He patted Obey on the shoulder. "You are the captain, Obey."

We all breathed out with relief. It would have been a horrible place for a fight. Especially a bat fight.

Obey smiled a tight little smile. He picked out of the bas-

51

ket the bat that George had just put back. It was long and heavy, even in Obey's big hands.

"We need a big bat," Obey said, and put it to one side. It was a masterful move. None of us dared look at George, and Obey didn't either. He just went on picking out bats. He did it scientifically. He picked a long and heavy (George's bat), then a short and heavy, then a long and a short medium-weight bat, then a long and a short lightweight bat.

It was well done and I saw Mr. Domres nodding his approval of the whole scene.

With the last bat picked and put to one side, Obey turned to Mr. Domres. "What happens when we break them?"

"Bring the broken bat back here and I'll try to fix you up with something. Though it probably won't be a new bat."

"You hear that, guys?" Obey said, turning to us. "Don't break bats. Anyone doesn't like any of these new bats can buy his own. You got no rule against that, do you, mister?"

"No," Mr. Domres said.

"OK," Obey said, "we're ready for our uniforms now."

"This way," Mr. Domres said.

We left the bat and ball section and went back to the shelves. As each guy came up, Mr. Domres and the kid who worked there handed him a cap, a shirt, a pair of pants, and a pair of socks. We were getting black caps and black socks.

It was all very formal and quiet until the guys started trying on their shirts and pants, and then it was chaos again.

"Trade with each other," Mr. Domres suggested, "till you get near your right size."

"How do I look?" Tidwell asked. His pants came down to his toes.

"You look like hell," George growled.

"I look like Aretha Franklin in a pants suit."

"This shirt comes down to my knees. I could wear it as pajamas," Tom said.

"Hey, what's this say? Billings Tool, who're they?"

The patches on the backs of some of our shirts said "Billings Tool."

"That was the name of last year's team. I've ordered Atlas Movers patches for you boys, but they haven't arrived yet. Soon as they do, I'll get them to Mr. Corkins and you get your mas to sew them on."

"Tidwell can sew them on for us."

"Shut up, Chico."

"What I do have here now is the schedules for the season. There are eight teams in the league, and you play each team twice. The team that's listed second is always the home team. There's a map on back that tells you where each park is. I've got a copy for each of you, so don't crowd up."

We crowded around anyway and got our schedules. The first thing I noticed was that West Park was our home park. The second thing I noticed was that we played back-to-back games with the bank team. They were the fourth and fifth games of the season. We played them first at West Park and then a couple of days later at Veterans Park, called Vets, where we were the visiting team.

"You'll notice all games start at 5:45 P.M.—"

"Hey, we play the bank the second time at 7:45," Claude said.

"Except for games under the lights," Mr. Domres finished.

"What lights?" Tidwell asked, a little nervously.

"We play under the lights?"

"Hey, like the pros."

53

"I never played under lights before."

"You got to wear smudge under your eyes."

"How many games do we play under the lights?"

"Two. Arborville Bank and Ace Appliance."

"Oh, man. I can't wait for that."

"How do you see under the lights?"

"With your eyes, Tidwell."

"I didn't mean that . . ."

"Men," Mr. Domres said, "I've got more teams coming in here to pick up equipment tonight, so unless you have any questions—"

"I got one," Obey said.

Everyone shut up.

"Do we get a chance to practice under the lights?"

Mr. Domres studied Obey for a second before answering, and then he turned to Pa. "You know, Mr. Corkins, I've been coaching teams for twelve years, and managing this league for three, and that's the first time anyone ever asked me that question. It's a darn good question, and the answer should be yes, but unfortunately it's not. It's not, because we have to share those fields with the Connie Mack League and the adult baseball leagues, not to mention the twelve, thirteen, and fourteen-year-old leagues. I have to fight hard just to get the few games there that we do have." He paused, and then added: "Sounds like you boys have got yourself a good field captain, though. Now, if there are no more questions, you can take off with your loot, and good luck to you this season. I'm glad we've finally got Sumpter Street in the eleven-year-old league."

"Good luck to you, too," Tidwell said, and we ran out of there, laughing, clutching our pants, socks, shirts, caps. Everyone ran except Obey, who was quietly carrying the heavy equipment bag.

We held a quick informal meeting on the grass outside the school.

"Who isn't going to be at practice tomorrow morning?" Pa asked.

No one raised his hand.

"Good. Anyone who needs a ride, come to my house at a quarter to ten."

"Everyone walks," Obey said, "it'll be good for our legs."

"Should we wear our uniforms to practice tomorrow, Mr. Corkins?"

Pa thought about it a second. "Well, you'll only be getting them dirty."

"That's OK, Coach," Obey said, "so we get them dirty. From now on, we wear our uniforms everytime we practice. We're gonna look like a real baseball team."

Obey was right. The Tigers practiced in uniforms. A real ball club wore uniforms.

On that note the meeting ended, and the guys took off through the streets, yelling and holding their uniforms over their heads as though they'd liberated them from stores on Main Street.

Obey and I carried the heavy equipment bag over to our car and put it in the trunk. Then Pa drove us home. The three of us felt so good about the way things were going, we didn't say a thing.

Tomorrow's practice would be even better.

SEVEN

UNTIL PA ACTED so peculiar at the end, it was a great practice. It was a beautiful morning for baseball, not hot, not cold. Just a little breeze. Kids were flying kites, playing basketball near the shelter. West Park is a big wild park with ravines and trees and hills, and you could hear kids on bikes chasing each other back there but you couldn't see them.

It was the kind of morning when even if you weren't a baseball player, you'd want to go out and loosen up your arm.

When Pa and I arrived at West Park at five minutes to ten, I didn't see the Sumpter Street gang at all. I saw a strange baseball team in sparkling white uniforms standing on our diamond. For a second I thought some wise guys had grabbed our field, but then I recognized Tidwell's ugly face under a black cap, and I realized it was us. The Atlas Movers, a new baseball team, playing for the first time in an organized league.

I wasn't the only one who felt strange about it. All the guys were acting funny, stiff, walking gingerly as though a button would pop if they ran.

"Ain't it something, Ezell?" Tidwell whispered to me as we unloaded the equipment bag.

"I know. I know."

Everyone stood around stiff and formal till Pa opened up the ball bag. Tidwell grabbed a white ball; Obey grabbed it from him and stuck it back in the bag. "That's a game ball, man."

"Obey," Les pleaded, "I never played with a white ball before."

Obey looked at him and saw Tidwell was serious. He patted Les on the shoulder. "You got lots of white balls ahead of you, man. OK, guys, loosen up."

We loosened up, and gradually the strangeness wore off. Obey had worked out a drill for us. Batting practice and then a fielding practice. Ten swings apiece. I waited for everyone to rush up to bat at once, which was how the old Sumpter Street gang would have done it. But the Atlas Movers in new uniforms waited for Obey to tell us how we'd do it.

"We'll bat around the infield," Obey said. "George, you'll bat first. Then Claude, Chico, Ed. Then Ezell, Tom, Tidwell. Then Gary. Then me. Tom, you'll pitch for Gary when he bats. Second time around it'll be five swings apiece. Tidwell, you'll play the batter's position when a guy bats."

Obey had planned it in detail. I was proud of him. So was Pa. Pa was pleased Obey was running it. Pa had laid out the batting helmets and the running helmets. He was starting to work on the bats. He enjoyed arranging the equipment.

"Hold on," Tidwell said, "I ain't gonna catch when you bat."

"Sure you will," Obey said.

"I'm not gonna catch Willets."

"Tom'll be pitching then. Ten swings the first time around. Bunt the tenth and run it out. Don't try to kill the ball either. This is a batting practice. Gary, don't burn them in. You're gonna pitch lots of pitches so just la-di-da them in there. Let them hit."

"Obey, I wanna fog a few through every now and then."

"You fog 'em through now and then and I'll fog 'em through you. You wanna bust your arm? Your arm's gonna carry us through the season. What do you say, Coach? How's it look to you?"

Obey had turned to Pa, who was now laying out the bats in a fan shape with all the handles coming together.

"Why, just fine, Obey," Pa said, smiling, "just fine."

"Any special instructions?"

"Just you boys do what Obey says. This is your first day, so don't sprain a muscle trying to kill the ball. Just meet it up there, like Obey says."

Obey clapped his hands. "Let's go," he said, and we gave a yell and ran out to our positions and then began our first and best practice.

It was beautiful. It was beautiful because Obey sang out from his catcher's position, taking charge of Gary, moving fielders around, talking to batters, telling them to bend their knees, stand closer to the plate or farther from the plate, tap the far end of the plate to make sure the pitcher couldn't cut the corner on them—that they were close enough.

And he sang to Gary and controlled the big guy, making him throw easy pitches and let everyone hit.

And everyone did hit. Bats rang out and balls flew to all corners of the field, and the guys ran out their bunts like lions were chasing them down the base path.

58

Obey made us all talk it up in the field.

"I wanna *hear* you guys," he shouted. "I cannot *hear* you guys."

So we sang.

"Atta pitch, Gary."

"Way to throw, Gary."

"Nice and easy, Gary."

"Hey, big Gary . . ."

It was only batting practice, but it was our first, and we'd waited all our lives for it.

In the field, we played our positions as though we'd been born there. Chico was as good as he said he was, Ed was a little better. George Copp knocked balls down with his chest, his shoulders, and hustled to touch the bag at first, hustling like he'd never even done on the basketball court. Claude was super at second, never a wasted motion. Tom Martin had to be the best eleven-year-old center fielder in America. He had real range and moved on the crack of the bat. I got off more slowly, but once I got to the right spot, I was all right.

When we were all through batting around the second time, Obey practiced special plays with us.

"Where're you gonna throw it? There's a man on first."

He hit the ball over shortstop. I ran hard, cut it off, whirled, and threw to third.

"Way to go, Ezell, that's throwing ahead of the runner. Man on second. Where're we throwing it?"

He hit a sharp ground ball to second. Claude scooped it up and threw to first.

"You mighta had a play at third," Tidwell yelled.

"It was two outs," Claude replied. "I just got the side out."

We laughed.

"OK, wise guys," Obey said grinning, "there's one out. One out. What're you gonna do with it?"

He chopped down at the ball and sent a high hopper down the third base line to Ed. It was not a good ball for a double play or even to get the lead runner, but Ed could have a chance for it if he charged the ball and short-hopped it. It would be a real gamble, because he could boot it, too. It was the kind of thing a third baseman has to make an instant nonthinking decision about. Ed decided to lay back, grab it on the second bounce, and get the sure out at first. He did just that, firing the ball across the diamond to George.

I thought it was the right play and I guess Obey did, too, because he didn't say anything about Ed not trying to get the lead runner. But then, all of a sudden, out of nowhere, my father, of all people, spoke up.

Up to now Pa hadn't done a thing except to clap his hands and cheer us on, and neaten up bats and balls and helmets that were already too neat. But now, out of nowhere, Pa came charging onto the field and began telling Ed Moore how he should have made that last play.

"Ed," Pa said loudly, "you got to move in on that ball and short-hop it if you want to get two. You can't lay back. Move in, boy. Give yourself the edge."

And then to my amazement and embarrassment, Pa bent down and started showing Ed Moore how he should have done it.

Obey's mouth fell open; the other guys just gaped. Poor Ed didn't know what to think. He just stood there, holding his glove, staring shamefacedly at the ground.

"Now that is how it is done," Pa said loudly, and I wondered if he had flipped, gone crazy. Things like that could happen. I heard of a man who was walking down Main Street one day and suddenly decided he was Jesus Christ and began blessing people. Here was Pa, up to now quiet and content, and then when Ed made a good enough play, he came charging out onto the field to give him a big lecture.

Finally the lecture was over, and Pa patted Ed on the rump and trotted off the field. As he did, I saw him look off to the right, toward the West Park shelter. I looked that way too. Standing there next to the water fountain was Mr. Robert Gardner and a kid our age who had to be his son Robby. They'd been standing there for I don't know how long, watching our practice. They'd come down to scout us and Pa must have spotted them and decided to put on a show for them.

"Oh, Pa," I said softly, miserably.

"Let's get going," Obey yelled. He hadn't figured it out yet, but Ed had. Ed saw the Gardners. Ed turned around and gave me a what's-going-on look. I shook my head, pretending I didn't know.

Pa waved at the Gardners and Mr. Gardner waved back.

"I guess you come down to scout us," Pa called out cheerfully.

Mr. Gardner frowned. "We were just driving by and saw you practicing. Looks like you got yourself a good ball club, Willie."

Obey got it then, and so did the others. Pa was pretending he was running things for the man. Obey got so mad he swung his bat and blasted a vicious line drive into the dirt at Chico. Chico got so mad he charged it, scooped it up, and fired a scorcher at George.

"Ouch," George said and fired the ball to Claude and

around the infield it went, the guys burning the ball at each other.

"Oh, the boys are pretty raw yet," Pa said loudly, "but I'm gonna whup them into shape. Yes, sir, Mr. Gardner, I'm gonna take these boys in hand."

No one said a thing. And then Obey, thank goodness, laughed. "You look kinda whupped in there, Chico."

"So do you, Parker," Chico snapped back.

"Let's see how whupped you look on this one, Moore," Obey said, and he hit a smash between Ed and Chico. Ed threw himself at the ball, knocked it down, and from a prone position he flipped the ball to Claude at second.

"I didn't say there was a man on first," Obey called out.

"You didn't say there wasn't," Ed replied.

The guys all laughed.

And Pa's crazy behavior was forgotten. Pa was forgotten and the man he was acting up for was forgotten. It was just going to be baseball, and that's what it was for them. They came all loose and could do no wrong. They turned Obey's base hits into double plays, and while it was only a practice it was a sign of things to come. I knew Mr. Gardner, being a vice-president of a bank, could read signs.

"You ain't seen half yet, Mr. Gardner," Pa yelled. "You got to see my boys hit. And watch big Gary pitch. That's Gary out there in right field now. He's got a hummer that'll burn you. Yes, sir. Gary has got speed. S-P-E-E-D. Stick around now, my boys'll hit some and I'll get Gary to throw his smoker—"

Stop it, Pa, I prayed. Stop it!

But it wasn't Pa who stopped it, it was Mr. Gardner, and he stopped it by leaving. He'd seen enough. He'd come down to scout us, not to get psyched out. He and his son left in a hurry.

The practice went on. And it was a good practice. But for me, Pa's funny behavior had ruined it. We weren't just a baseball team for Pa. We were an instrument of revenge. I felt uneasy about the future.

EIGHT

THEN THERE WERE the games. At first there were practice games which we won easily. In a game against Baer Machine, Gary struck out nine straight guys. Tom pitched a three-hitter against Mallory Metals two days later, while Obey and George hit back-to-back home runs. We played a final practice game against Ace Appliance, who had finished second to Arborville Bank last year, and we beat them 2-1 in a squeaker.

The day after the Ace Appliance game, Pa came home and announced that Mr. Gardner was worried about us. "He has heard about our exhibition victories, sure enough," Pa said. "In the parking lot, he give me the fishy eye."

"And just what does a fishy eye look like, Mr. Corkins?" Ma asked.

Pa glared at her. "Woman," he said, "it looks like the eye of a man that knows he's gonna be cooked and ate real soon."

Even Ma had to laugh at that description of the vice-president of a bank.

The following Monday we opened our real schedule

against Claymore Restaurant at Stone School field. Claymore wasn't very good, but we helped them by being nervous. If it wasn't for Gary fogging pitch after pitch past them, we would have lost that game. As it was, we finally woke up and realized their rinky-dink pitcher had nothing on the ball. We were just overanxious at the plate. So we started waiting on his pitches. Obey showed us how by banging a triple in the fifth. George singled him home, and then Ed Moore hit a home run down the left field line. Before that inning was over we had six runs. Tom mopped up the last two innings.

Gary had two innings of eligibility left on Thursday when we played Farm and Garden. They were a well-coached team, but without fire. Maybe they were too well coached. Their coach in the third base coaching box sent so many signals down to the batter that those kids were thinking up there instead of swinging. Tom pitched a six-hitter and we bunted and singled a good fast-ball pitcher of theirs to death. That was the game in which we learned how to use our speed to intimidate another team. Everyone except George Copp was running. We had those kids making tags before they caught the ball. We had their catcher throwing down to second before he had a ball in his hand. We forced their good pitcher into two balks. We just rattled them, and when it was over we'd won 5-2.

Monday after that we had our first good crowd of spectators at Sampson Park when we knocked over Ace Appliance. I guess word had got around that a hot new team was in the league, and kids from other teams that weren't playing that day, as well as a lot of Ace Appliance parents, came out to watch. We had squeaked by Ace in the practice game, but we were all done squeaking now. We jumped their pitcher for five runs in the first inning, two of them un-earned, when their left fielder let Obey's line drive single go through his legs.

Obey started Tom. He wanted to save Gary for the bank team on Thursday, and Pa said that was a fine idea. Tom pitched for five innings, and though they hit him in every inning, our infield was really terrific. Chico, in particular, had a fantastic day, going into the hole in deep short, and making the long throw to George on target. He had a good arm. Obey finished off things in the top of the seventh by hitting a solo home run, a blast over the left fielder's head, and Gary struck out the side to end the game.

One thing Obey was proving over and over was his boast that baseball was his game.

After we shook hands with the Ace kids, Pa made us hud-dle for a quick meeting. He told us that while we were going great now and were undefeated and all that, nothing really counted till now. Thursday we were playing the champs, the bank team. It was also our first home game, and Pa wanted us to get our folks to come to this game.

"We ought to have fans," Pa said, " 'cause they will have them. I want to hear a lot of cheering for us, too."

"It won't do them no good, Mr. Corkins," Gary said. "When my old smoke comes in there, they'll wish they never came."

Pa just couldn't get a real pep talk going without Gary or Tidwell making it sound funny. But Gary wasn't trying to be funny. He was serious. He felt he was God's gift to pitch-ing. And I guess that was one reason he was so good out there. Pitching is a lonely job and pitchers think like loners, and the pitcher who'll beat you is that pitcher who thinks like a cocky loner. Like he was born to beat you.

66

That week was also the last week of school, which is always a crazy week. Mrs. Hadley had a terrible time keeping order. Tidwell in particular was jumping up and down telling everyone how he'd hit a double in the last game, where the ball had gone, and how he'd slid into second under the tag.

Claude told him he wasn't going to hit any doubles off Robby Gardner's curve ball on Thursday.

Obey said anyone's curve ball could be hit, you just had to either wait for it to break or get up in the batter's box and hit it before it broke. I don't know how Obey knew things like that, but he did.

Everyone had suggestions about how to hit Robby Gardner's curve ball except Mrs. Hadley, who suggested we be quiet if we wanted to get promoted into seventh grade. We were quiet for a while.

That week the Atlas Movers were the talk of the sixth grade, and a whole bunch of kids wanted to join our team. But Obey wasn't eager to have them. He said we needed insurance players and one of these days he'd hold tryouts. But for now we had all we needed, nine guys.

Obey was cocky, and Obey was wrong, because after our first big game with the bank team, we needed another ball player—to replace Obey.

NINE

I HAVE SINCE found out that everyone has different ways of getting rid of his nervousness before a big game. Tidwell does it by talking. Talking about anything, not just baseball, but movies, TV shows, what his Uncle Mike keeps in his pockets, why oak trees are no good, why the river smells. Obey doesn't talk. He's the opposite. When he's nervous he goes out and shoots baskets alone. He won't even play in a game. He just wants to shoot alone. He says all the butterflies in his stomach fly into his muscles and flow out his hands into the ball and they leave him when he throws the ball into the air.

Tom goes to the toilet a lot; Claude says he doesn't get nervous. Ed Moore claims he beats up on his kid brother. George Copp eats cookies. Chico stares at his hands; Gary throws stones at stop signs.

I read. I find I can get out of my skin by reading, I guess because reading puts you into someone else's skin. Like the day of that big game against the bank team. When I woke up a soft rain was falling and I thought, no game today. Was that good or bad? Did that mean a Saturday makeup game? Then the rain let up, but it stayed overcast and drizzly, and I thought they'd play. I was certain they'd play and I might as well not think about it and read. Gray days are good for reading anyway, so I could kill two birds with one stone. Use up a gray day and get rid of my nervousness.

I picked up Laughing Face again and started reading. Between school and baseball I hadn't got too far in it, but school was over now and baseball wasn't till 4:30 or so, so I had a whole day to read. Laughing Face was a lot older now in this chapter and he was supposed to become a brave.

I was just starting to read that, a million miles and a million years away from Arborville baseball, when I heard my father come up the front steps.

I looked out the window. It was drizzling slightly, and Pa had walked home under the big old bank umbrella which he is supposed to use to escort bank customers from their cars to the bank and back again. It's blue and yellow and says ARBORVILLE BANK on it.

I looked at my clock. It was only 3:45. Even on the day of a game, it was too early for Pa to come home. My mother thought so, too.

"Mr. Corkins," I heard her say, "what on earth are you doing here at this hour?"

"Well," Pa said, "I saw Mr. Robert Gardner leave the bank to get ready for the game, so why shouldn't I?"

"Did it ever occur to you, Mr. Corkins, that he is a vice-president of the bank and that you work in his parking lot?"

"Woman, don't rile me up on the day of a game. I got to concentrate on baseball."

"Oh, my heavens, I am married to a lunatic. I hope you make a lot of money coaching children's baseball after you are fired from your job, Mr. Corkins. And please leave that umbrella outside. It doesn't even belong in our house."

69

"I will bring it back in the morning," Pa said. "Where is Ezell?"

"Upstairs reading, and please let him read."

"How can he read on the day of this game?" Pa asked.

"Perhaps there will be no big game, Mr. Corkins. It *is* raining."

"We will play," Pa announced. "The rain is stopping and the field will be dry in an hour."

I heard Pa come up the stairs.

"Where are you going, Mr. Corkins?"

"I got to talk things over with Ezell," Pa said. "How he can read before a big game I do not know . . ."

I guess I knew then and there how Pa got rid of his nervousness. He gave it to other people. No sooner had he found out that I was reading calmly then he came into my room and made me put Laughing Face away, and he started going over the bank team. Did I know this one and did I know that one, and had I seen Robby Gardner's curve ball, did it curve in or out, and did he have a fast ball to keep you honest and was it as fast as Gary's, and was their number two pitcher Norm Burns, who was also their first baseman, any good, and did I think we could run on their catcher or bunt on young Gardner, and how did I feel? Was I nervous?

By the time Pa got through with me, I was nervous.

Worse yet, it had stopped raining, and we would play. Which was too bad, because it would have been a lot better for us if that game had been rained out.

TEN

TO EXPLAIN WHAT HAPPENED in that horrible game, I've got to describe West Park in more detail than I already did. West Park is the oldest park in town. It has got hills and woods and ravines in it. Years ago a stream ran through it, but it has long since gone underground. It's a real wild-looking place. On the only level piece of ground in the park, the city built the baseball diamond. It's a good diamond. Except for the newer diamonds at Veterans Park, it's probably the best diamond in the city. It's got one big problem, though. It's sunk lower than the rest of the land, and it's also surrounded by trees. Because of that, it gets darker earlier on that diamond than it does elsewhere. You can still finish a game in daylight at 8:00 P.M. at Buhr or Sampson, but at the West Park diamond you're in the darkness. This, plus the fact that the day was overcast to start with, made it get darker even earlier the day of the game with Arborville Bank.

Pa and I hadn't thought this far ahead when Ma drove us to the park a little after 4:15. I was annoyed about getting there that early, especially since Pa had told the guys

71

they didn't have to be there till 4:45, but Pa said he wanted to check out the condition of the field.

I was sure no one would be at West Park that early except the pigeons, but I was wrong. The whole Arborville Bank team was on the field having a batting practice, and all our guys except me were on the bench watching them.

"The early bird catches the worm," Pa said softly. "Only now it looks like a real fight 'cause we got two early birds."

"How do they look?" I asked Tidwell, who came over with Chico to help us unload the equipment.

"Good," he said.

"Just fair," Chico said.

"How's the diamond?"

"Good," Tidwell said.

"Just fair," Chico said.

"You guys would make a good comedy act."

"Nothing to laugh at," Tidwell said, "they got a good team."

"Warm up," Pa said, "loosen up those arms."

Pa spoke loudly and I knew he was talking for Mr. Gardner's benefit as well as ours.

While we warmed up, I watched the Bankers practice. Mr. Gardner was pitching. They had an enormous number of players, and none of them at first glance looked bad. There were a couple of big guys there. Norm Burns, their first baseman, was big. So was their catcher. Robby Gardner was my size—middlin'. He was the only one seated on the bench, chewing gum and watching the batting practice. He was wearing a warm-up jacket. Mr. Gardner took care of his pitchers.

I was interested that he and Pa hadn't said hello to each other. It was a big game, all right.

I noticed, too, their guys were really smacking the ball around. Mr. Gardner wasn't putting too much on his pitches, but they were still smacking away. Were they putting this show on for our benefit? Did they always have a hitting practice before every game like major leaguers? We should have scouted them.

"We're here early enough," Chico said. "Are we gonna have a batting practice, Obey?"

"Yeah," Obey said. "Mr. Corkins, ask that guy Gardner when we can have the diamond."

Pa looked at his watch. "Let's give them a little more time, Obey."

I wondered about that. Each team had to have about ten minutes of infield and outfield fielding practice. That, plus talking over the ground rules with the umps, staking bases, etc., would take us practically up to game time.

We gave them more time and kept warming up. I threw with Tidwell and Ed Moore. Pa laid out the equipment, the bank team banged the ball around for our benefit, talking it up, and the stands slowly began to fill with people. When people came to a game a half hour early, you knew this game was being talked about. Arborville Bank had been undefeated last season, they were undefeated this season. We were the hot new team, the unknown quantity; this was a showdown game early in the season, with a second game scheduled for Monday.

"How about the diamond now, Mr. Corkins?" Chico asked.

Pa pushed his porkpie back and scratched his forehead. "Well . . ."

"*I'll* tell him we want it," Obey said bluntly.

"No, I'll tell him myself," Pa said.

We stopped warming up to watch Pa walk up to the third

base foul line and try to get Mr. Gardner's attention. Mr. Gardner didn't stop throwing. He ignored Pa. Mr. Gardner wore a red cap, a warm-up jacket, slacks, and baseball shoes. He looked like a suburban coach. Pa wore his porkpie, an old fishing jacket, street shoes, and regular pants, and he looked like . . . well, he looked like Pa.

"Say . . ." Pa said.

"Hello, Willie," Mr. Gardner said, without looking at Pa. He threw to the plate. The batter hit a hard ground ball to third. The third baseman grabbed it and fired across the diamond. A nice play. The third baseman had nice hands. Ed Moore couldn't have done it any better.

"Say," Pa tried again.

The batter bunted the next ball and took off. The catcher pounced on it and whipped it down to first. Another nice play. It was obvious now they were putting on a show for us. There's nothing quite like trying to beat a team before the game starts.

"Tell him we want the field," Obey said loudly. Loud enough for Mr. Gardner to hear.

"You want the field, Willie?" Mr. Gardner asked, and I could see a tiny grin on his face. I knew right then and there I hated that man.

Pa nodded. He was flustered. He didn't know how to handle it. I closed my eyes. I wished I were a million miles away. I wished I were reading about Laughing Face; he at least could handle his problems alone. He didn't have a pa he had to feel funny about.

"Yes," Pa said, "we want the field."

"A couple more and you can have it, Willie."

That "Willie" was like a slap in the face. Pa knew it and we knew it.

"Nice guy," Ed Moore murmured.

"A sweetheart," Tidwell said.

"A couple more and it'll be game time," Tom said.

"What's the rule book say about this, Ezell?" Obey asked.

"Doesn't say anything. Rule book doesn't say he has to give us a crack at the field at all. Leastways not hitting practice."

It was clear to us all Gardner wasn't going to give us a turn on the field. It was also clear that Pa wasn't going to stand up to him. Maybe Pa was saving it for the game. I hoped so.

Finally, with only about twenty minutes till game time, Mr. Gardner turned and offered us the field. What he was offering us was ten minutes of fielding practice, and it meant he'd want ten minutes, too.

"Let's go, boys," Pa said grimly. "Let's hustle out there and show *them* a thing or two."

"Hold on," Obey snapped.

We hesitated.

"Let them have the infield practice first. We'll wait till the umps get here with the bases."

It was smart thinking. It was a lot better to practice with bases than without. But I guess Mr. Gardner was ahead of us there, too. He had his team running off the field and sitting down on the bench, and Pa was faced with the job of telling Gardner to get his team back on the field.

"Go ahead, Willie," Gardner shouted across the diamond at Pa, to make it a little more difficult, I guess. "It's all yours."

"The louse," Tidwell said.

"Tell him to get back on it, Mr. Corkins," Chico said.

Pa sighed. "Let's go, boys. Let's save our ammunition for the game."

Obey looked at me; I looked away.

"C'mon," George Copp said, "let's show those kids who we are."

We took the field. The whole thing was not right, but it wasn't all wrong either.

"Hit 'em around hard, Obey," Claude said.

"Obey, you catch," Pa spoke up. "I'll hit them around."

Obey froze. Before every game, it was Obey who had given us infield and outfield practice. Now Pa wanted to do it. I knew why, and so did Obey. Let him, Obey, I prayed. Just this once.

Obey handed him the bat. "Go 'head, Coach," he said.

I prayed Pa would look good hitting to us. It would pick him up, give him something to fight Mr. Gardner with if trouble arose during the game. And at first, he did look good. He hit some hard grounders to the infield, and the guys fielded well and threw well and we all began to pick up, to talk a little.

But when it came to hit the ball out to us in the outfield, Pa had a hard time. It took him five tries to lift a fly out to me, and when he did, some wise kid on the bank bench yelled: "Hooray."

Pa was flustered, but he kept trying. He got a fly ball out to Tom after three tries and one out to Tidwell after three tries. It slowed up the tempo of the practice, it took us down. The infielders stood around glumly. Pa got back to hitting them to the infielders when the umps arrived and began staking bases, right in the middle of our practice. It seemed like everything was going wrong. I didn't know yet that worse was to come.

We had to give up the field to the bank team, and while Gary and Obey warmed up, the rest of us watched Mr.

Gardner give his team fielding practice. On their sideline, Robby Gardner warmed up with his catcher. He had a nice compact motion, not as big as Gary's; he wouldn't throw as hard as Gary, but it was controlled and all within him. It didn't look like anything would rattle the Gardner kid.

On the field, the bank team looked sharp. Neat, compact, flawless. They were well trained. They talked it up. They looked like skilled ball players rather than natural ones. They had style. But there was no Chico or Ed Moore out there. There was no Tom Martin in the outfield, and no one as imposing physically as George Copp. And certainly their catcher wasn't in the same league as Obey. He was big but he threw stiffly. We could run on him, if we could get on base.

But the Bankers had pep and organization and Mr. Gardner gave them a snappy drill.

"Play for one.

"OK, now let's get two.

"OK, outfield, look alive.

"Man on first, Dennis, where're you throwing the ball to?

"Let's get two. Let's get two.

"Who's got it? Call for it. Make it loud.

"Who's covering on a bunt?

"Two men on, where's the throw going?

"Let's get the sure out. The sure out."

Even though I hated the guy, I had to give him credit. He put his team through a fast-paced fielding drill, simulating a game, and he picked them up so that they were singing all the way. It was just the opposite of our fielding practice. And our guys sat on the bench in silence and watched. Pa sat there silently too. Were we beaten before the game started?

The umps signaled for a coaches' meeting. Obey always

went up with Pa, but this time Pa told him to keep warming up Gary.

Obey took a deep breath. I thought he was going to explode, but he didn't. He just turned away and went on warming up Gary. I walked over to him. Gary's fast ball smacked into his glove.

"It'll be all right," I said.

"You think so?"

I nodded.

"I don't," he said.

Obey whipped the ball back. I stood there watching him and Gary, and then Pa came back and called us over. He pushed his hat back. "OK, boys, here're the ground rules. Ball goes into the ravine in deep center on a fly, it's all you can get. Ball goes in on a bounce, it's a double. Out of play is either side of the backstop. They're up first and they're ready to be taken. We're gonna run on them, hit them, really take them apart. Right?"

The words were right, but the feeling wasn't there.

Tom turned to Obey. "What're the signals going to be?"

"Same as last game," Obey said. "Take off my cap is steal. Take sign is hands on hips. Bunt sign, touch right toe. Wipe off all signals, I end up touching both elbows."

"Good," Pa said. "Now I want the batter and the base runners to be looking at me before every pitch—"

"Where're you gonna be, Mr. Corkins?" Tidwell asked. We were all surprised.

Pa grinned. "Why, I'm gonna be coaching at third, Mr. Tidwell."

"But Obey coaches third."

"Not this game, Tom. This game I want a hand in the victory."

All the guys looked at me. I knew they expected me to

talk my pa out of this. He couldn't coach third. He'd never coached third. Coaching is a hard job. It's thinking fast, thinking ahead. But how was I gonna tell Pa he couldn't do it? I thought fast and had an idea.

"Pa," I said, "I forget the signals. Could you go through them again for me?"

I knew he didn't remember them. Maybe he'd take this hint.

"Let's see, take sign is touch. No, that's not it, is it?"

"It's hands on hips, Pa."

"Right, touching both toes is a steal."

"Steal is taking off your cap, Pa."

"Ezell, why're you asking me this if you remember it all?"

I almost laughed. It was awful and tense and I almost laughed. "Pa, it's you who got to remember, not me."

"Ezell, if I forget I'll call the batter over and tell him what I want him to do. Besides, you boys don't need signals. You're the most natural bunch of ball players I ever seen in my life, and I seen a lot of great teams. You don't need me to tell you to steal, take, hit . . . you can do this by yourselves. Those boys are a bunch of machines over there; you are free-wheelers. Be free-wheelers. Run them to death. You win this game for me, boys, and we'll be eating pizzas afterward. All the pizzas you want. So get out there and hit the ball and run. They've never seen kids fly the way you kids can fly. So fly on them. Gary, I never seen a better young pitcher than you in all my life. I'm gonna sit back and enjoy watching you blast them over the plate. They're nothing, that bank team. All style, that's all. They're not hungry. We're hungry. We've been waiting for years to eat them up, so get there now and take them. You hear?"

It should have been a great pep talk; it should have sent

79

us charging out there. It didn't. Pa had a crazy gleam in his eyes. No one dared look at him. He was talking to himself.

"You still think it's gonna be all right?" Obey asked me, as we left the bench.

"I don't know," I said.

ELEVEN

IT WAS GOING to be awful. But not right away. Not with Gary Willets pitching. Gary's fast ball would make us look good for four innings.

They had never seen anything like it. The first three Arborville Bank kids came up, and the first three Arborville Bank kids went down. Only Robby Gardner swung at the ball and he missed it by a mile.

It felt better running in. If Gary could keep us in the ball game till we got ourselves together, then maybe . . .

But we hadn't figured on Robby Gardner being that good. He was. Maybe not quite as good as Gary, but good enough to make us look silly. He had a fantastic curve ball. Chico fell in the dirt chasing it, and when he came back to the bench he threw his bat down disgustedly.

"Tough, huh?" Obey said.

"No," Chico said, "he can be hit but you got to go with it."

"Either that or get up front," Obey said.

We watched Claude bat. It was a repetition of what just happened to Chico. Claude chased three curve balls and ended up on the ground, with the bank team laughing and zipping the ball around and their parents in the stands clapping.

Obey slid the doughnut off his bat. "What do you think?" he asked Tom. "Up front?"

"Got nothing to lose."

I knew what Obey was going to do. He was going to stand way in the front of the batter's box and try to hit the curve before it broke. I was sure we'd learn how to hit it. The trouble was, this was the first time any of us had batted against a good curve ball. Gary didn't throw a curve, Tom threw a little one. But the Gardner kid really broke one off.

Obey stepped into the batter's box and you could feel everyone in the stands grow quiet. They knew who Obey was. He had a reputation already, partly because of his older brothers. Parker boys from Sumpter Street were all natural ball players.

Obey had a natural batting style, too, feet apart, relaxed bat, eyes intent on pitcher. He could concentrate the way none of us could. He also had bat control. He didn't swing till the last second, and he could hit the ball where he wanted to. Because Obey stood away from the plate, I guessed Gardner would try to feed him a curve over the outside corner. It looked like Obey was giving away the outside corner, but he wasn't really. He had measured it, tapping the far side of the plate with his bat.

Robby Gardner tried anyway, aiming for the outside corner with that low curve. Obey reached out and hit the ball . . . foul down the first base line. It was solidly tagged.

You'd have thought he hit a home run by the way we reacted, jumping up and yelling. It sounded good, wood against ball. Obey stepped out of the batter's box, got some dirt on his palms, rubbed it in, and then stepped in again, way up front. Robby Gardner studied him. Then he nodded to his catcher, wound up. I thought the curve would come again, but this time it was a fast ball. I didn't know he had a fast ball. It was sneaky fast because it came out of the same motion as the curve. He threw it again for the outside corner, hoping to sneak it by Obey, who was up front looking for the curve. Obey hit it and hit it again down the first base line, foul. It was a line shot. Gardner watched it go, and so did Obey, and then the two of them looked at each other. Obey was grinning a little, Gardner wasn't. He just chewed his gum.

Obey stepped out and rubbed some more dirt on his palms. It was no balls and two strikes. Obey was deep in the hole, but from the way he acted, the way he took his time, he made it appear that now he had Robby Gardner just where he wanted him.

Obey stepped back in, only he backed up a little in the box. He was going to have to guard the plate now. I noticed he moved in a little closer, too.

Gardner pumped and threw a fast ball. Obey went up for it, and then pulled his bat back at the last second. It was outside for a ball. Only a kid with great eyes and bat control and confidence could do that.

"Way to look, Obey," George called out.

Gardner fussed around the mound. Obey just watched him, bat resting on shoulders. When Gardner was ready, Obey crouched; his bat came off his shoulders an inch or so. He waited and watched. Gardner threw another fast ball. Obey held up again at the last second. It was low and inside for a ball.

"C'mon, Ump," Mr. Gardner shouted, "the plate's got corners."

"So's your head," Tidwell called back.

"Shsh, Les," Pa said.

83

Obey stepped out and rubbed more dirt. He was waging a war of nerves with Robby Gardner. But Gardner looked nerveless to me.

Everyone was quiet. It was a real duel.

Gardner's next pitch was a curve, and Obey went for it and pulled it foul down the third base line. Obey could hit his curve, he could hit his fast ball. It was encouraging for us all.

Two and two, Gardner threw another curve down low. Way low. No doubt about that one.

"Way to go, Obey," we called out.

"Good eye."

"Make him pitch to you."

"He's your meat, Obe."

"He's scared now. Hey, pitcher, you're sweating now."

But if Robby Gardner was scared or sweating he didn't look it. He turned his back on Obey and rubbed the ball up. Obey stepped out and played games with the dirt again. Pa looked nervous. He clapped his hands and touched his elbows but none of it was signals. He was just nervous.

Finally Gardner was ready, and Obey stepped in casually. I figured Gardner to throw his fast ball. Three and two, Obey had been timing the curve. He'd try to nip a corner with the fast ball. Low and away. That was how I figured it and I figured wrong. Obey, who didn't do any figuring, like any good batter with plenty of confidence in his reflexes, just stood there waiting, and when Gardner gave him the big motion and came down with a slow gutty three and two curve, he was waiting for it. You could see him wait and wait and wait until you couldn't stand it any longer, and I felt like shouting: "Swing, Obey, swing."

Obey swung. The ball smacked out of there like a bullet.

We yelled and then swallowed our voices in a thick silence.

Their second baseman came out of nowhere, dove for the ball, knocked it down, and lying flat on the ground threw out Obey by a step. It was a great play. A great pitch, a great hit, a great play in the field.

It was great baseball, and their fans applauded.

Pa shook his head. "We'll get him next inning," he said.

"Lucky," Chico said.

"Way to bang 'em, Obey."

Obey was disgusted. "I hit it right at him."

That was Obey for you. But the fact was, he'd picked us up. Gardner could be hit, and we would hit him. We trotted out onto the field feeling better and better. We were a lot closer to hitting Robby Gardner than they were to hitting Gary.

While Obey put on his equipment, Pa warmed up Gary, and that was when Ma and the twins arrived. I saw my mother give a double take at Pa catching, but when she saw Obey putting on his gear she figured it out. What my mother didn't know about baseball was a whole lot.

The second inning was the same as the first. Gary fogged it by the Bankers and struck out three more guys in a row. Their bench was real quiet and so were their fans. We talked it up in the field.

But in our bats, we didn't do much better. At least we hit the ball, but always at someone. The curve was hard to time. We popped up, grounded out, and flied out. Both pitchers had no-hitters going.

One thing good was that the game was moving along quickly. I didn't think darkness would be a threat. One worry was that Gary only had five innings of eligibility, and someone said that Gardner had seven. They'd saved him for this game. Maybe. But I didn't think Mr. Gardner would use him all seven, seeing that they were going to have to face us again on Monday . . . but you never knew.

In the bottom of the third, Obey asked Pa to check with Mr. Gardner how many innings his son could pitch, but Pa said it didn't make any difference 'cause if he pitched all game today they couldn't use him Monday. Pa was right, but I knew Obey felt the real answer was he didn't want to check anything with Mr. Gardner. And Obey was probably right there.

In the top of the fourth, either Gary lost some speed or they were beginning to time his fast ball. Each guy got a piece of the ball. The top of their lineup was up. Their number one guy hit a hard ground ball down to short. Chico gloved it easily and threw him out, but it was the first solid sound off their bats all day. Their next guy worked Gary for a three and two count and then hit a long fly to center. Tom was under it easily. Gary looked annoyed with himself, but he bore down on Robby Gardner and got him on a high pop-up to first.

Still, you could tell the bank bench was encouraged. They started yelling at Gary, telling him his shoelaces were untied and dumb things like that. Gary didn't listen to them. He knew pitchers had to turn off bench jockeying, and he was able to.

In contrast, we seemed to get feebler against Robby Gardner. Chico struck out for the second straight time, so did Claude, and Obey worked Gardner to a three and two count again and then popped up to him.

They were a lot noisier than we were, as if they knew they were going to get to Gary before we bothered Gardner. We talked it up, and sang, and told Gary it was a breeze, but I think each of us was beginning to have some doubts.

Gary had trouble with the first two men in the top of the fifth. Their number four batter Norm Burns worked him to three and two before he hit a line drive into right field. Tidwell was there and caught it.

Their number five man laid down a bunt. But Obey was on it and whipped the ball to first, and he was out.

"Two down. Way ahead, Gary. Nothing to worry about. Don't listen to their bench. They're nothing. All mouth. All style. It's like shooting down ducks, big Gary. Picking peaches. Strolling home. Just fire, big boy. Just fire."

Well, he fired, and the ball went in the dirt and skidded past Obey. It was the first really bad pitch Gary had thrown all day. And I thought I knew why it had happened. Some part of Gary's pitcher's mind had figured out he was going to have to strike out everyone; he was going to have to win this game himself, and now he was trying too hard. He was pressing. And his rhythm was gone.

Obey called time and went out to talk to Gary.

The bank team jeered both of them.

Obey patted Gary on the rump and went back behind the plate.

"Two away, Gary," Chico yelled. "Just fog it by him."

"Pitch to my glove, Gary baby," Obey called out. "My glove, my glove, my glove . . ."

But Gary couldn't find Obey's glove. Sailing along on top of the world, he was now suddenly adrift. He walked the kid on four straight pitches. The bank team started pounding bats and yelling at Gary.

Obey called time again, and they started yelling: "Stall."

Though why Obey would want to stall was beyond understanding. Darkness wasn't a threat yet. We weren't winning. It was just something to yell, I guess.

He and Gary talked it over again and then Obey returned to his position.

"Two out," Claude called out. "Forget about the guy on first, Gary."

But Gary couldn't forget about him. He didn't pitch as well from a stretch as he did with a windup. The kid danced off first trying to distract him. Gary threw to first, and the ball almost got away from George.

"Pitcher's going up, up, up, up . . ."

"Work on the batter, Gary."

"We're behind you, Gary."

"Airtight, baby, airtight."

"To my glove, Gary. To my glove."

"You got him, Gary. Your meat, Gary."

"Hey, pitcher, pitcher, pitcher, pitcher . . ."

"Going up, up, up, up . . ."

Gary threw two more balls and Obey called time again.

"They must like to talk."

"Don't you guys know each other?"

"Hey, they're real friends, aren't they?"

"Shut up," Gary said to their bench, and this made the bank kids talk even more.

"Ignore them," I heard Obey say. "They're all mouth . . ."

The whole infield came around. I looked over at Pa. It was probably inconceivable to him what was happening now, Gary blowing up. No one ever figured Gary to blow up. Pa just sat there, shoulders slumped, hat back, and watched.

The plate ump broke up the meeting. Gary walked around the mound, examining it, as if the cause of his wildness could be found in the dirt.

Then he looked over at the kid on first, who wiggled his

hands at him. Baby stuff, I thought. Then he looked at
Obey who held up two fingers for everyone to see. "Two
outs, guys," Obey said, "let's get the easy out. Forget about
the kid on first. Pitch to me, Gary. To me . . ."

Gary checked the runner on first and threw in the dirt.
The runner took off. Obey knocked the ball down and
threw. It was a beautiful low hard throw, but the kid was in
ahead of it. Chico took a swipe at him anyway with his
glove, and they all started yelling: "Throw him out."

"That's no way to play ball, shortstop," Mr. Gardner
shouted at Chico.

"Lawyers," Tidwell yelled.

Some of their fans booed. Gary was shook up. I looked at
Pa. He was looking at his score sheet.

We all knew what was going to happen next, and it did.
Gary threw ball four. Obey called time again and set off the
usual holler from their bench about stalling and meeting,
and didn't our pitcher and catcher know each other, and all
that old garbage.

Gary was kicking at the mound, and Mr. Gardner, to add
a little fuel to Gary's fire, called out: "Easy out there, boy. I
got a pitcher has to use that hill too."

"Ah, shut up," Tidwell yelled.

Mr. Gardner looked at Tidwell and then at Pa on our
bench. Pa was busy pretending he hadn't heard Les.

"What do you say, ump?" Mr. Gardner asked the plate
ump, and the plate ump went over to talk to Pa. I could
guess what he was saying because I'd seen it in the rule
book. Kids who got on adult coaches could be thrown out of
the game. If Tidwell was thrown out, we'd be playing with
eight men. Which you could do if the other coach gave his
permission. I couldn't see Mr. Gardner giving that permission.

The ump was warning Pa, and Mr. Gardner was huddling with his next batter, and Obey and Gary and the infield were talking together. I took the opportunity to run over to Tidwell and tell him he could get thrown out of the game for yelling at that coach.

"I don't like him," Tidwell said.

"I don't either, but I don't like losing to him either."

Tidwell kicked the ground. But he got the point.

"Batter up," the ump said.

All the meetings broke up. Obey went back behind the plate. Their batter, their number eight hitter, stepped in. He couldn't be a very good hitter if he was batting eighth. Gary didn't have to burn it past him. All he had to do was get it over the plate. We would do the rest. But old Gary had one speed: fast.

He threw his smoker. To my amazement, the kid just extended his bat over the plate. He didn't even try to swing. He just stuck his bat over the plate. The ball hit the bat and looped into right field.

Tidwell came charging in, but the ball dropped in front of him. Les did well to knock the ball forward, keeping it in front of him. Their runner from second scored, and the guy on first was scrambling for third. Les threw too late to third. Chico smartly cut it off at short, hoping for a play at second, hoping the kid who got the fluke hit would be trying for two. But the kid was jumping up and down on first, yelling happily. A fluke hit could do a lot for some kids. But was it a fluke? Or had they discovered a way to hit Gary's smoker? Let the smoker hit the bat and bounce around for cheap singles.

The bank bench was yelling. They were throwing their gloves in the air as though they'd just won. Gary stood out

90

on the mound, and he looked plain defeated. All the cocki-
ness was gone from his shoulders. That was a good pitch
he'd just thrown. Right on target. And a puny hitter had hit
it. I wondered if Pa would come out and talk to him, but Pa
still wasn't moving.

Mr. Gardner was moving, though. He was whispering
something in the ear of his number nine hitter, probably
telling him to do the same thing. To let the ball hit his bat.
Not to swing. Then he sent the kid up.

Obey squatted down. "Lucky hit, Gary, lucky."

Not so lucky, I thought. Take something off it, Gary, I
whispered to myself. Don't throw it so hard. This guy's their
weakest hitter.

"He's finished, Jay. He can't pitch anymore."

"You'll need a ladder, Obey."

Gary looked in for his signal, which was no signal at all
because Gary was only throwing one pitch this game. Pa, I
thought, go out there and tell Gary to take something off his
pitch. Call time and tell Gary it's batting practice. At least
make them earn their hits.

But Pa just sat on the bench and looked worried. Gary
was his big pitcher. Gary was the boy who could hit a stop
sign with a stone at sixty yards. Gary would see us through.
Pa, please. Please, Pa, go out and talk to him. Pa—

"Ezell!" someone shouted.

Yells, screams. I looked up. I was asleep. The ball was
coming out toward me. The kid had hit a soft pitch. It was
coming toward the foul line, in fair territory. Oh, you fool.
Asleep. Run, run . . . you've got to catch it.

But I started too late. I got the tip of my glove on the ball
and it rolled off. I ran back to get it. The kid on third had
scored, and the runner from first was rounding second,

heading to third. I fired the ball low and hard to Ed Moore. It came into his glove on one bounce. Ed grabbed it, spun, and put the tag on the kid.

"Out," the ump shouted.

We yelled instinctively, but the damage was done. Another run had scored. We were down two runs against a pitcher who was getting stronger and smarter as the game progressed. I had personally given away the second run by trying some ESP on my Pa to get him moving when I should have been trying ESP on myself.

I came to the bench not looking at anyone. Someone muttered: "Good throw, Ezell," but there was no heart in his voice. I sat down at the far end of the bench and looked down at the ground.

"Martinez, Claude Martin, Parker," Pa called out, and a second later I felt his hand on my shoulder. "That was a mighty fine throw, Ezell."

I shook my head.

"We'll get those runs back, won't we, boys?"

No one said a thing. Gary kicked a bat. "It's my fault," he muttered. "I had it and then I lost it. I just lost it."

"What'd you lose?" someone asked.

"My rhythm, that's what."

"We got a dancer pitching for us," Tidwell said.

Gary jumped up. George stepped between them.

"Let's bloody them, not us," Tom said.

"Maybe we ought to stall," someone said. "It's starting to get dark."

"Is it an official game, Ezell?"

"Yeah," I said. "Four innings make an official game."

"Let's not stall, let's beat them."

"How, man, how?"

"Jump that dinky curve. That's all it is, a dinky curve.

We're not attacking it. We're watching it and worrying it and we're not jumping it."

"I didn't see you jumping it, Obey," Tidwell said.

"I'm gonna, though," Obey said.

"Batter up," the ump said.

"Let's go, Chico. The guy's got nothing on the ball. Bang it, man."

It was Chico, Claude, and Obey. One, two, three. Top of the batting order. One, two, three they came up, and one, two, three they went down. Obey attacked the ball OK. He just didn't hit it.

Robby Gardner was a tough smart pitcher.

"You think you can hold them, Gary?" Ed asked.

"How do I know?" Gary said, discouraged.

"You only got one more inning to pitch," Obey said. "Just chuck it in. Ezell, you stay awake."

"I will."

"Boys," Pa said, "I know we're gonna get to the secret of that curve ball next inning."

"If there is a next inning," Tom said gloomily. We all looked at the sky. It was getting dark fast. And since it was already an official game, time was running out on us.

TWELVE

NOW COMES THE awful part of the game, and the worst
moment in my life.

Gary didn't settle down in the top of the fifth. He walked
a guy; the next guy tried to bunt the man ahead and spent
forever at the plate. Finally he started swinging with two
strikes on him and began fouling off pitches. We had two
game balls, and at one point both balls were lost with everyone searching for them.

All the while, time was being used up, and now it was
getting dark. Not real dark yet, but I knew in a little while
it would suddenly get dark, as though someone in the sky
had drawn a shade and said: NO MORE BASEBALL!

But that didn't happen yet. First Gary had to kick dirt
and go to a three and two count on everyone; and balls had
to be lost, searched for, and found; and Mr. Gardner had to
whisper instructions in every batter's ear. He wasn't in any
rush to finish the game. It was clear to everyone we weren't
going to get a full game in. One more inning at the most. So
we had one more lick at bat to catch up and beat these
guys.

They didn't score in their bats, but they used up a lot of time. And finally we were in for the bottom of the fifth.

"Let's hustle, guys," I said, "we got to score fast now."

It was really getting dark now. That big shade in the sky was coming down.

"What'll they do?" Tom asked me.

"Call the game. It's an official game now."

"Do we play it off later?" Claude asked.

"Nope. Rule book says if a game is called early for any reason and it's past the fourth inning, making it an official game, then the score goes back to the score of the last completed inning."

"So we got to get runs and beat them and end the inning," Claude said.

"Right."

"Let's go. Let's hustle. Who's up?"

"Copp, Tom Martin, Moore, Willets," Pa called out.

"Let's jump this guy."

Obey got hold of George and was whispering something in his ear. George nodded. Pa clapped his hands. "Hit away, big George," he called down.

The bank team talked it up in the field. No one had said anything about it getting dark now. But everyone on both teams was thinking about it.

Robby Gardner took his time. He didn't hurry his warm-up pitches.

"C'mon," Obey shouted, "let's get the game moving. It's getting dark."

"Our pitcher's got to warm up," their third baseman said.

"Stuff it," Tidwell said.

"Batter up," the plate ump called out.

George stepped in there and I noticed he was swinging with a choked bat. Obey's instructions. Probably to shorten the swing. Do to them what they'd done to Gary. Just hold the bat out and chop at the ball. The ground was darker than the sky. A ground ball would be hard to see. Neither of the two game balls was particularly white. Of course, a dark ball was hard to hit too. It was equally dark for both teams.

Robby Gardner fussed, took his signal, went to a full windup and threw his curve outside. George almost went for it and held up.

Gardner then threw another curve outside. He took his time between pitches, and I knew then I wasn't the only one who'd read the rule book. So had Mr. Gardner. He and his team were putting on the stall. Gardner must have told his son to waste pitches, which wasn't all that smart, since it's not always easy to get them in when you want to.

And that's what happened. Robby Gardner threw two pitches wide, and then his father yelled out: "OK, Robby."

Robby nodded that he understood, and he threw ball three and then ball four, and believe it or not we had our first base runner of the game. It was our turn to make noise now. Pa in the third base coaching box was sending George all kinds of signals which George had the good sense to ignore. Obey, who was coaching at first, having made the last out in the previous inning, was, I hoped, telling George not to steal. George was slow. Besides, it wasn't George's run we needed, but Tom's.

"Give it a ride, big Tom."

"He's your baby, Tom, boy."

Tom stepped in, but just as Robby Gardner was about to pitch, his father signaled for time and came out to talk with him.

"Now look who's stalling," Tidwell said.

"Hey, Ump," Claude shouted, "let's move it along."

The sky was a deep dark blue. I joined the chorus on the bench. "Let's go. Let's move it. Let's get the ball game going."

The plate ump came out and told Mr. Gardner to hurry it up. I heard him say it was getting dark and he wanted to get the whole inning in. Mr. Gardner said sure, sure, he'd hurry, but he stayed out there and chatted with his son, and then he walked slowly back to his bench.

"Batter up," the ump said, even though he didn't need to since Tom was in there already. But Robby Gardner wasn't ready to pitch. He had to move dirt around with his toe, then stare at George at first. Finally he put his foot on the rubber, took a signal from his catcher, looked over his shoulder at George and back at Tom, and then he threw over to George. George wasn't even taking a big lead. But that didn't prevent Robby Gardner from throwing not once but three times. And the third time he threw, George was standing on the bag all the time.

We were mad all right, furious, yelling "Stall."

Finally Gardner pitched to the plate, outside, as though it was a pitchout and big George was going down. George just stood on the bag and the catcher made one of those I-dare-you-to-go motions and finally threw back to the pitcher while we hooted. But time was running out; it was getting dark, and in the stands the fans were shouting things like:

"Hey, turn on the lights."

"Who's got a candle?"

"Can't tell the players without a searchlight."

"It's getting pretty dark, Ump."

The ump ignored the fans. Tom dug in. Gardner pitched home, wide. I don't think he meant to throw it wide, but all this clowning around, the phony throws to first, had

97

knocked his rhythm out of whack. It was all going to back-fire on the Gardners, father and son.

Robby was beginning to crack a little, he kept looking nervously over at his father. He was a marionette, worked by his old man.

Finally, Robby aimed a meat ball and Tom stepped into it. It was our first hit of the game. A smash over the short-stop's head. George rounded second and headed for third. The left fielder had the ball. He could have tried for a play at third. He might have had George, but he smartly whipped the ball to second to keep Tom on first. It was Tom's run that scared them, not George's. Tom's run would tie up the game. Then the ump could call it on account of darkness, and we could play off from scratch another time.

Now our side was on their feet yelling, shouting at Ed Moore to knock in the runs. Ed was a clutch hitter. He was a solid pull hitter. Have you ever noticed how many third basemen pull the ball to left, down their own line? I don't know why that is, but it just is.

Pa was talking to George, telling him to be careful, not to get picked off, but to go on a ground ball. Obey was talking to Tom and I could guess he was telling Tom, who was re-ally fast, to go down on the first pitch. They wouldn't risk a play at second with George on third. We were going to bust it wide open. If Robby Gardner would go ahead and pitch. But their catcher wasn't in any hurry. He looked over at Mr. Gardner and then called time and ran out to the pitch-er's mound.

We hollered, but it didn't do any good. Their shortstop and first baseman came over for the conference. Mr. Gard-ner didn't come out. If he had, it would mean he had to yank his son. And he wasn't ready to do that. Not yet.

"What do you say, Ump?"

"Let's go."

Our shouts were met with shouts from the stands.

"Turn on the lights."

"Call the game."

"Make them play, Ump," I shouted.

"It's too dark to play."

"Nuts to you," Tidwell shouted.

Finally the ump broke up the conference at the mound. And now it was really dark. It wasn't pitch black yet, but it would be awful hard seeing a ground ball. A ball hit up against the sky could be seen, but I bet it would disappear against the tree background as it came down.

Ed waited at the plate, calm, efficient, chewing gum.

Gardner looked over at third and then he threw to the plate. Tom was off on his motion. No one could catch him, not even a major league catcher. The ball was outside. The catcher straightened up and pretended he was firing to second, but in reality he was only firing it back at the pitcher. Robby Gardner caught it and was ready to throw home to catch George, but George wasn't moving. It wasn't his run we needed but Tom's, and now we had Tom on second, nobody out, and the whole game was turned around. Now if only Ed could bust one before the ump called the game.

"Time, Ump," said the loud voice of Mr. Gardner, and he came out on the field. We groaned. There was nothing we could do, for he announced: "I'm changing pitchers, Ump."

"Better hurry, Coach," the ump said, "it's getting dark."

He didn't hurry, though. Gardner brought in Norm Burns, his first baseman, to pitch. He moved his son to short, put his shortstop in center, and brought his center fielder in to play first.

"Why don't you put your catcher in right and let your

right fielder catch," Tidwell yelled. "That'll use up more time."

"Easy, Mr. Tidwell," Pa said.

"Pa, make them speed up."

"I can't, Ezell," Pa said. "He's got to warm up."

"Six pitches," Obey called out. "Only six pitches."

Mr. Gardner laughed at Obey. "You want someone to get hit. It's hard enough for the batter to see the ball as it is."

Norm Burns warmed up slowly. In the outfield, their new center fielder warmed up. At shortstop Robby Gardner was fielding ground balls from the new first baseman. It was frustrating.

In the stands, the fans were now openly yelling for the umps to call the game. "Someone's going to get hurt, Ump," one shouted.

The ump ignored them. He was only sixteen and showed a lot of courage, I thought, with all the adults shouting at him. He knew fair was fair and that we were coming back, and it would be unfair to stop the game now. We had the momentum now. We were going to beat the bank team and everyone knew it. Even the bank kids knew it. They were leading by two runs, but they were quiet. The game was slipping out of their hands.

Finally the ump called for Ed to step in. Mr. Gardner said one more thing to his pitcher, patted him on the rump, and walked slowly off.

Norm Burns was a big kid who looked like he had a fast ball.

Sure enough, he threw a fast ball inside for a ball. Ed looked down to Obey at first for a signal. Obey was telling him openly to swing away. A hit meant two runs. It meant a new ball game.

Norm Burns went to a full windup, almost daring George to steal home, but George wasn't moving. Burns threw a blistering pitch. Ed swung and was way under.

"Only takes one, Ed," Obey shouted. "Only takes one."

The strike picked up the Bankers and they started chattering. Norm Burns checked George and then fired again to the plate. Ed crossed up everyone by bunting. It caught George and Pa by surprise.

"Run," we screamed.

George took off, late. It was a beautiful bunt down the first base line. Their new first baseman was playing back. Norm Burns had to make the play himself. He had George dead out at home, but George was big and could barrel into the catcher, and suppose the ball started bouncing around behind the backstop? I don't pretend Norm Burns thought all those things in that instant. I know I would have thought them; I did think them as a matter of fact, but Norm did the smart thing. He let George score, he faked a throw at first and then he whipped the ball to third base hoping to catch Tom making a big turn. It almost succeeded. The only reason it failed was that his third baseman wasn't expecting the throw, and he dropped the ball. Tom dove head first back into the bag. It was a very smart fielding play that almost broke the back of our rally. But it hadn't worked, and now there was nothing to stop us. Gary was up now. Gary could hit. No one out; we could beat the darkness now. Only one more run to tie it up, and one more to win it. We weren't playing for a tie anymore, we were playing for a victory.

"Time, Ump," came the loud arrogant voice, and there came Mr. Gardner, holding up his hands in a T, coming onto the field.

There wasn't a thing we could do to stop him. The ump

couldn't stop him. Someone turned a flashlight on in the stands. "Hey, Ump, use this light to help the kids see."

The ump was getting shook now. It was dark. He took off his mask and came down the third base line to talk to Pa.

"I think it's too dark to go on, Coach."

"Let's finish this inning," Pa said.

"This inning could take another twenty minutes," the ump said.

"We're goin' as fast as we can. It's him that's stalling."

"I know he is, but he's got a right to talk to his pitcher."

"You got to give us more time, Ump."

The ump was undecided. He went out to second base and talked to the bases ump. And then the two of them came back and the plate ump told Pa he'd give us five more minutes.

"You can't play baseball against a clock," Pa protested.

But the ump shook his head. "It's too dark to play now," he said. "Five minutes. Let's play ball," he called, and went back to home plate.

I went over to Pa.

"What is it, Ezell?"

"Tom's got to steal home, Pa."

"You think so? Gary can hit."

"It's too dark to take a chance. Send Tom on the first pitch."

Pa nodded. "Maybe you're right. You think I should ask Obey?"

"There's no time."

Obey was way across the diamond, coaching first; he was looking at us, and I knew he'd approve.

Pa went over and whispered to Tom. Their third base-man looked at them and then he shouted out: "Watch out for the squeeze."

Squeeze? We hadn't even thought of Gary bunting. Some brainy coaches we were. It didn't make any difference. Gary couldn't bunt. It was too dark to bunt. All Gary had to do was get out of the way.

"Five minutes, Coaches," the plate ump called. "Let's go."

Mr. Gardner was still out at the mound. He was talking earnestly to Norm Burns. "C'mon," Tidwell yelled, "get off the field."

Mr. Gardner ignored him. Norm Burns nodded. He didn't look happy. Finally Mr. Gardner left, and a hush grew over the field. It was eerie—the sudden silence, the darkness, the dim white shapes of the outfielders. It was too dark now to even see a ball hit against the sky.

Gary stood in there. He knew Tom was coming down. He kept glancing at Tom, who was taking a long lead off third. Their third baseman was in close, expecting a bunt. He'd promoted the idea himself. If he laid back, he could have kept Tom close to third.

Norm Burns went to his stretch position. Ed Moore broke for second. Robby Gardner bluffed toward third, Tom had to go back. But Norm Burns had to throw. He would have balked if he didn't throw. Tom cut for the plate and Norm Burns threw, and that was when we found out what Mr. Gardner's strategy was, why Norm Burns had looked so unhappy. He'd been told to hit Gary with the pitch. And he did. The ball hit Gary just as Tom slid across the plate and Gary and Tom were tangled in a heap. The ball rolled away. It was a dead ball. No play. A hit batter. Gary would have to go to first. Tom would have to go back to third. Bases would be loaded, nobody out, and more time used up.

I was aware that my name was being screamed.

"Ezell, get up there. Move it, Ezell!"

103

It was Obey telling me to get into the batter's box. I jumped for a bat. But I needn't have hurried. Gary was still on the ground, and Tom was angry at being told to go back to third. Obey then took charge. He gave Tom a shove to third; he practically pulled Gary along to first. Gary kept saying his arm hurt and Obey kept telling him to shut up, it wasn't his throwing arm, and yelling at me over his shoulder to get in there and hit the ball.

I stepped in.

"Ump," came the now familiar voice of Mr. Gardner. "Ump, that kid never saw the ball coming. It's too dark."

"You threw at him on purpose," Tidwell screamed.

"Batter up," the ump said. But I was in there already. The bank kids weren't in position, though. They had started to come in when Mr. Gardner yelled that it was too dark to play.

"Get back out there," Obey said to them.

"Shut up, Parker," one of them said.

Obey drew back a fist, but he checked himself.

"Son," Mr. Gardner said to the ump, "you'll be held responsible if one of these kids gets hurt."

The ump was weakening. Mr. Gardner turned to my father.

"We just had a warning. Willie, you don't want your son getting hit on the head. It's not worth it. It's just a ball game, isn't it, Willie? What do you say, Willie?"

"Let's play," Pa said.

"How about your five minutes, Ump?" Mr. Gardner said.

"You used up four by yakking," Chico said.

"Watch yourself, son."

"You go watch your own self, mister."

104

The ump looked at his watch. "You got one minute left. One more minute."

"Make it one more batter," Obey said. "They'll stall a minute."

"They're stalling now."

"One more minute. Is it OK with you, Coach?"

The plate ump looked at Pa. And there it was, all wrapped up in one big question to my father. Pa could have said: "No." He could have insisted it be one more batter. He could have, but he didn't.

"Willie," Mr. Gardner said, coming over to Pa and putting his arm around him as though they were friends, "it's a tough one. I know. But it's not worth the risk of someone getting hurt. We better call it. It's just too dark. Look at it."

Pa looked and it was dark. It was night. He was going to agree.

Just then Obey yelled: "Let's play. One more batter. Let's go."

"You're not the coach, Parker," Mr. Gardner said. "Willie, what do you say?"

Pa nodded. "It's too dark," he said quietly, sadly.

And that was it. A dozen gloves went up in the air. The bank kids yelled jubilantly. The plate ump looked relieved. And then one of the gloves came down on Obey's head. He turned and belted the nearest bank kid to him. The kid went down. Another kid jumped Obey, and Tom jumped him, and a free-for-all started. Pa was yelling for us to stop. Mr. Gardner was trying to separate kids, but guys were rolling on the ground together, punching at each other. Both umps were in the middle trying to break it up.

Someone in a bank uniform came up to me. It was

Robby Gardner. He looked at me and I looked at him. Everyone else was fighting but us. The coaches' kids. I didn't want to fight him. I wasn't mad at him. I wasn't mad at anyone. It was all so rotten and mean; it made you feel sick, not angry. This wasn't how baseball should be. If this was what organized baseball was about, I didn't want any part of it.

Robby Gardner's hands were doubled into fists. He waited. I realized then I still had a bat in my hands. I dropped the bat.

"Go ahead," he said.

"You start," I said.

But he didn't start, and I didn't either. We just looked at each other and then he walked away, into the noise and the yelling and the darkness. I went back to our bench and sat down. As far as I was concerned, this was the end.

THIRTEEN

FOR ONCE, my mother had the sense not to say a thing coming home. She drove quietly. When we got home she put the twins to bed. The twins were half-asleep already, thank goodness. Pa kissed them good night and then he went out onto the back porch and sat in his old squeaky rocking chair.

Ma came downstairs and asked me if I was hungry yet and I told her I wasn't.

"You haven't eaten since lunch."

"I'm not hungry."

"I've got some chicken legs warming up for you and your pa."

"I'm not hungry."

"Well, maybe your pa is. Ask him if he's hungry."

The back porch was dark. Pa just sat in the dark rocking on the old linoleum floor that squeaked even if you just walked over it barefoot.

"Pa?"

He didn't answer.

"You hungry, Pa?"

"No."

"Ma's got chicken."

"I ain't hungry."

"Me neither."

I stood there, waiting for him to say something, but he didn't. He just went on rocking.

"You all right, Pa?"

"Yeah," he said, and spat through the crack in the screen door. "I'm all right. But you boys are going to have to get yourselves another coach."

"Are you quittin'?"

"Uh huh."

"Me too."

Pa turned and looked at me in the dark. "You? *You* didn't do anything wrong, Ezell."

"I don't like it, Pa. It's not sport. Everyone screaming at you. Adults and everything. It's no fun. I'm gonna quit too."

Pa was silent. "You quit, Ezell, and we won't have a team. We'll be short a man."

"I don't care."

" 'Course you care."

"I don't. I hated it. I hate that Mr. Gardner, Pa. I hate him. I hate him."

"Shsh, boy. Shsh. You don't hate anyone."

"I hate him."

I was suddenly crying. I don't know why I started crying, but I was crying. Pa got up and came over and put his arm around me and pressed my head against his chest. His old jacket smelled of fish and the river. It didn't smell of baseball. It smelled of good things.

"You all right now, son. That thing is over."

But I went on sobbing. Pa led me over to the rocker and

he sat down and pulled me onto his lap like I was a little kid.

"It's all over, Ezell. We got to live to fight again, don't you know? I been thinking this out, here in the dark. I been thinking about what happened and how I let the man beat me tonight. 'Course that is what he did. He beat me. It was getting dark and someone could've got hurt. *You* could've got hurt, but I let him beat me just the same. And I been thinking mighty hard why and I think I know why, Ezell, I think I know why. I been askin' you boys to do my job. I been trying to get back at the man through baseball, and it's got nothin' to do with baseball. Isn't that right, Ezell? You're a smart one. You read a lot. You knew what was happening. Wasn't that happening tonight?"

I nodded. Pa wiped my face with his hand.

"Yes, sir," Pa said softly, "from now on I fight my own battles. And I'm not gonna quit our old team. I may be the worst coach in America, but I'm not goin' to let the man push me out. And you won't quit either, will you, Ezell?"

"No, Pa."

"There, that's better. You all done crying now, aren't you?"

"Yes, Pa."

"Crying's good for the soul. Washes out your insides. That's what your grandma used to say. Now listen here, we got to talk baseball just for a second. You think we still got a team left?"

"I don't know, Pa."

"We got to find out right away."

"I'll go over to Obey's."

"You do that. We don't make a move without Obey. Now you wipe your face off in the bathroom. I don't want

109

your mother to think I been takin' a strap to you. Go 'head now."

I went into the bathroom and washed my face off and dried it. I looked at myself in the mirror. I looked strange to myself. Someone with big round eyes who looked older than he usually did. Well, I thought, you saw a lot of things tonight, and none of them you liked.

When I came out, Pa was in the kitchen. "We're goin' to eat a little supper together now, Ezell. When I married your mother, it was cause she was such a good cook. No other reason."

"Why, Mr. Corkins, I do believe you thought I was a good-looking woman."

"Love is blind, woman. Don't you know that?"

Ma laughed. She looked at me and I knew Pa had told her I was crying. She smiled at me.

"Well, now," she said, "you're going to get your strength back by eating. And then when you get your strength back, you are going to get your team back. And when you get your team back, you are going to wallop the daylights out of that Gardner bully and his mean little team. And I am here to tell you I am going to round up every woman in this neighborhood to go to the next game and cheer for you."

Pa winked at me. "Look out for her, Ezell. She's got blood in her eye."

Ma did look kind of grim. And just her looking that grim made us both feel better. For a couple of defeated old ball players, we did pretty well by her chicken. How you can be crying your eyes out one second and eating chicken legs the next is beyond me, but there we both were with my mother, of all people, telling us how we were to beat that bank team on Monday, and us eating chicken as though we were starving hungry. Which we were.

After supper, feeling a lot better, I went next door to find out how Obey was feeling.

Mrs. Parker answered the doorbell, and when she saw it was me she didn't say anything but just studied me for a second, as if she was looking for some kind of answer, which, I found out, she was.

"Come on in, Ezell," she said after a moment, "I want you to tell Mr. Parker and me just what happened in that game. Obadiah refused to eat. He just stomped around the house cussin' and swearin' and I told him to leave. Now we have to know what happened."

Mr. Parker was seated at the kitchen table drinking a cup of coffee. He was an older man with big powerful shoulders and soft eyes. He'd been a great athlete a long time ago. He didn't talk much, but you could see how strong and fast he once must've been. Obey and his brothers got their abilities from him.

Mr. Parker smiled at me. "Had yourselves a ball game, did you, Ezell?"

"Yes, sir."

"An' you lost, didn't you?"

"Yes, sir."

He smiled. "I told Obey he's got to learn to lose just like you got to learn ball to win. But he wasn't listening very good tonight. Was a bad one, huh?"

"Yes, sir."

"What happened?"

I didn't really want to go through it all again, but they were looking at me, waiting, and I knew I had to. For Obey's sake too. So I told them the whole story. I just left out one thing: my being asleep in left field and giving them their second run. But I told about the fight. I didn't tell how a glove had landed on Obey's head and he swung first. I just

111

said everyone started fighting at once, which is what you would have thought if you hadn't seen the glove land on Obey's head.

When I was through, Mr. Parker shook his head. "Good thing he ran out of here before I found out about that fight."

"Now, Arthur, he wasn't the only one fighting."

"There's a time for fightin' and a time for takin' your lumps like a man. That's what he's goin' to have to learn to do. How's your pa feel, Ezell?"

"OK . . . now."

"Maybe I'll go over and say hello to him. It's no fun coachin' when things like that happen. It's a lonely job anyways. You goin' out to find Obey now?"

"Yes, sir."

"Tell him to get home. Tell him his pa wants to talk with him."

"Yes, sir," I said, but inside I thought: No, I won't do that. I'll just be getting Obey in trouble with his pa on top of everything else.

"Before you go, Ezell," Mrs. Parker said, "take a cookie."

"I just ate, ma'am."

They smiled at me, they knew I wanted to get out of there. "Take some cookies for the twins, then," Mrs. Parker said.

I started to say they were asleep, but I realized she knew that. This was her way of thanking me for coming over and telling them what had happened.

"Thank you, ma'am," I said, and she gave me six cookies, enough for three sets of twins.

"You're welcome, Ezell. You goin' to the library tomorrow?"

Tomorrow was Friday. I'd even forgot there was such a thing as a library.

"Yes, ma'am."

"Take Obey with you."

I grinned. "It could be hard."

"If anyone can do it, child, you can. He respects you."

Not after tonight, I thought, but I nodded and said I'd try. Then I ducked out.

I was pretty sure I knew where Obey would be. Where the rest of the guys would be. The playground. That's where we went to lick our wounds. No Gardners, no umps, no adults came after us there. I figured the whole team would be there, sort of drifting over there.

What I didn't know was that I'd be walking in on a secret team meeting.

At night the playground isn't much. In fact, it's nothing. It's not even open. You have to climb a wire fence to get in, but once you're inside there's nothing to do except jump on the teeter-totters and try to balance them standing up, or run up the slide. If there's a good moon you can try to play basketball by moonlight, but the neighbors don't like the playground being used at night and they usually call the police.

The guys were all there, though. I heard them as I came up to the fence. They were on the teeter-totters, which were squeaking noisily. The guys were talking quietly. I climbed the fence and dropped down onto the grass on the other side. I hadn't meant to sneak up on them. I was going to call out to them, to tell them I was there, but the first words I heard—and it was Obey talking—stopped me in my tracks.

113

"I'm tellin' you," Obey was saying, "I can get my brother Lee to coach us."

"You're crazy. He don't even live around here, Obey." That was Chico.

"He'll come in for games."

"Suppose he won't. Then we forfeit or something."

"What about your pa, Obey?"

"He won't coach."

"Did you ask him?"

"No, but he won't. Not with Mr. Corkins next door . . ."

There was a silence.

"Seems unfair anyway," George Copp said softly. "Just because of one game."

"Only the biggest game," Obey snapped. "And he couldn't stick up for us. He works for that bank coach and he let him run the game."

"Can't blame him much for that," Claude said. "I don't know what I'd have done."

"I can tell you what I'd have done," Obey said angrily. "I'd have told Gardner to go chase himself."

"Yeah, you're eleven years old."

"So what?"

"So a lot. Mr. Corkins can't do that."

"Right. And that's why I'm sayin' he shouldn't coach us. We got to play them again on Monday. What's gonna happen on Monday? The same old thing. Then what're you gonna do? Cry in your beer?"

"Aw, cut it out, Obey."

"No, I won't," Obey said. "I'm not playin' if Mr. Corkins is our coach. It ain't fair. I'm not gonna play for a guy who won't stick up for us. And Ezell too. I didn't see him fightin' either, did you?"

"Come off it," Claude said. "Ezell's no fighter, an' you know it."

"There comes a time when a guy's got to fight for his team. Mr. Corkins didn't fight for us and he won't. Next game that Gardner is gonna run all over us again. Hey, Willie this, and hey, Willie that, and Mr. Corkins saying yessir, nosir, anything your big fat self wants, sir. And they take the ball game away from us again. I say we get another coach."

"Who?"

"My brother Lee."

"We been that way before, Obey. He lives in Detroit."

"One of Tidwell's uncles then."

"Funny," Tidwell said.

But no one had laughed.

"Maybe it'll only happen with the bank team," Tom Martin said. "Otherwise, Mr. Corkins lets you run the team, Obey. Doesn't he?"

Obey didn't answer.

"Let's take a vote."

"On what?"

"Whether we look for a new coach."

"That's a dumb thing to vote on, Claude."

"We ain't voted in a long time," Tidwell said. "Let's vote."

"This is the vote," Claude said, "whether we stick with Mr. Corkins or not."

"Wait a second. Ezell isn't here."

"He's gonna vote for his dad. We'll just count that as a vote for his dad."

"I don't know about that," Tom said. "I don't think Ezell likes his old man coachin'."

"He's got sense," Obey said.

115

I stood there in the darkness and thought I ought to tell them I was there. It wasn't fair hiding on them like this, but I couldn't do it. I guess I'd been there too long to announce my presence now.

"Let's vote," Tidwell said.

"All right, you first, Les," Claude said.

"I say stick with Mr. Corkins. We wouldn't've had a team without him in the first place."

Good old Les.

"Chico?"

"I like Mr. Corkins. I felt sorry for him tonight."

"Ed?"

"I don't care."

"Gary?"

"Long as I get to pitch, I don't care either."

"How's your arm feel?"

"It hurts, man. It hurts."

"Shut up, you guys, we're taking a vote."

"George?"

"I say stick with Ezell's pa. He didn't lose us the game. I didn't see none of us power hitters doin' much powerin' at the plate."

"George's right," Tom said. "Maybe we're blamin' Mr. Corkins for what we didn't do."

"I'm for Mr. Corkins too," Claude said. "Let's see . . . that makes five in favor—"

"Six with Ezell."

"Six in favor. Two who don't care. And what about you, Obey?"

Obey was silent.

Claude said: "Where're you goin'?"

"The other way from you," Obey snarled.

I saw a figure go over to the fence, climb it, and drop down the other side.

"Well," Tidwell said, "that takes care of that. Now what?"

"We can't play without Obey," Tom said.

"Maybe we ought to ask his brother Lee to coach."

"Who's gonna tell Mr. Corkins?"

"What'd we take a vote for anyway?"

"Let's work it out in the morning. Copp, which one of us is gonna get off the teeter-totter first?"

"Me," George said, and jumped. Chico came down with a thud, and then he started chasing George all over the playground. While the rest of the guys cheered him on, I quietly climbed back over the fence and walked home.

"Did you get to talk to Obey?" Pa asked me.

"I couldn't find him."

"You'll find him in the morning," Ma said.

FOURTEEN

WHEN THINGS ARE BAD, I like to sleep. When you're asleep, you got no problems. You don't need to find solutions to problems you can't do anything about.

The next morning I slept as long as I could. When I woke up, it was raining. I lay there in bed listening to the sounds of the rain running through the gutter over my window, and then I closed my eyes and forced myself to fall asleep again. I don't know how long I slept, but the phone rang downstairs and suddenly my mother was shaking me.

"Ezell, it's nine o'clock. You're going to get the sleeping sickness if you keep this up."

"It's raining out, Ma. Why do I got to get up? It's vacation."

" 'Cause you got to take the bank umbrella to your father. He forgot to take it back this morning. Hurry now."

I groaned. Pa and his absent-mindedness. And of all the things I had to bring back to the bank for him, I hated the umbrella the most. I hated it the first time I saw it, which was in a newspaper ad. There was a picture of Pa posing under it with a bank customer. The caption under the picture read: ANOTHER PERSONAL SERVICE FROM

THE ARBORVILLE BANK, and then it went on to say how Mr. Willard Corkins, who directed the bank parking lot, was now running a free umbrella escort service in rainy weather for bank customers.

It was bad enough to see it in the paper, worse to see Pa using it in his parking lot, but really worst when he brought it home with him and then forgot to take it back, like now. And now it was raining and some of the bank's precious customers were getting their heads wet.

I dressed and went downstairs. The twins had their dolls all over the kitchen floor. I tripped over a Raggedy Ann and got mad and gave it a good kick. It sailed into the living room for a three-point field goal.

Louisa bawled: "Mama, he kicked my doll."

Marie said: "I'm gonna kick something of yours."

"Yeah, what's it gonna be?"

"You," she said, and kicked me in the shins. I smacked her on her behind and sent her sailing into the living room after the doll. And she started crying too. It's really great being an older brother to twin girls. They stick together and you end up in the soup.

My mother came into the kitchen. "Why did you kick Louisa's doll?"

" 'Cause I almost broke my neck on it. She leaves it anywhere."

"Couldn't you have picked it up and put it in the living room? Or are you too tired after your fifteen hours of sleep?"

"Aw, Ma."

"Don't 'aw Ma' me. And why did you kick Marie?"

"I didn't kick her; she kicked me."

"Why is she crying then?"

" 'Cause I hit her."

119

"Oh, for goodness sake, Ezell. Eat your breakfast and take the umbrella down to your father before you make any more trouble. And you better take an extra umbrella for yourself."

"Today's Friday. I'm going to the library."

"Good."

I ignored the taunts of the twins and had some juice and cereal, and then I got out the stupid old bank umbrella from the front closet and my ma's little blue one.

"Mean guy," Louisa said.

"Ratfink," Marie said.

I faked a kick at them. They squealed and fell back on top of each other. I got out the front door fast before they could get me in any more trouble.

It wasn't raining hard now. Just steady. I'll say this much for the big bank umbrella. Nothing got through it.

I walked by Obey's house. He was probably sleeping. I wondered if he felt bad about quitting the team. Knowing Obey, he probably didn't feel a thing. He only cared about one thing: winning. Obey couldn't be on a losing team. Pa wasn't a real coach; even he knew that now, but Obey hadn't got any hits off Robby Gardner himself. But without Obey we couldn't have a team. It wasn't just that he was a ninth man; he was our leader.

I walked up to the corner of Fourth and Sumpter, and then I saw something on the next block that really surprised me. With the rain coming down steadily, a lone wet figure was on the basketball court in the playground, shooting jump shots. It was Obey Parker himself: bareheaded, wearing sneakers and a windbreaker, ignoring the rain.

I stood there and watched him. When things get too tough, I sleep; Obey shoots baskets.

I walked up to the playground and then went inside it

120

until I was only a few yards away from him. He didn't turn around; he didn't look at me, but he knew I was there. All good athletes have eyes behind their heads.

Obey shot, and the ball rolled off the rim. He followed it up, jumping, getting a palm under it in midair, hanging up there, and tapping it up and in. It was an incredible kind of thing for a kid our age to be able to do.

Obey picked up the ball, held it in both hands, and twirled it between his fingers. He looked at me and at the umbrella. Then he nodded, turned, and was about to shoot again.

"Obey."

"What?"

"Are you quittin' the team?"

He looked at me. "How'd you find out?"

"I heard." Which was the truth.

"Yeah," he said, "I'm quittin' the team."

He shot and missed. The rain was coming down harder now.

"We won't have a team without you."

"Tough."

He missed a lay-up. Puddles were forming on the court.

"You're gonna ruin your ball."

"What's it to you? It's my ball."

"We can't play without you. You're the captain."

Obey turned angrily. "I was some captain last night, wasn't I, Ezell? I *really* ran the team last night." The rain was running down his face; he looked wild. "When we formed the team, you said I would coach the team and your pa would manage. You remember?"

I nodded. Had I said it? Or had I let other people say it? It didn't matter; it was what we all had felt.

"But that ain't what happened last night. Your pa let the man walk all over him. Didn't he?"

I nodded.

"He didn't walk over me. He walked over your pa. Your pa gave him that game. Your pa's the coach. Not me. Ain't that right?"

I nodded. I didn't know what to say. Pa was the coach. We could call Obey coach all we wanted to, but in the crunch, when a decision had to be made, the umps would go to my pa.

"That's right," Obey said. "Your pa's the coach and he can't coach. He can't stand up to the man. What's gonna happen Monday night, Ezell?"

"I don't know."

"I do."

"You don't."

"Yes, I do. If there's a fight, your pa's gonna give in to him. He works for him. And where's that leave us? Shoot . . ."

He stood there, and the rain was coming down really hard now and Obey was just getting wetter and wetter. But I had the feeling he wanted something from me. A guy doesn't get this mad in the rain without wanting something. He wanted me to tell him Pa wouldn't let it happen again, that Pa would stand up to Mr. Gardner. But I couldn't tell him that; I didn't know that.

"Bull, I say. Bull, bull, bull. . . ."

Obey turned and shot hard through the rain. The ball didn't come anywhere near the basket. It hit off the backboard and rolled toward me. I put out a foot and stopped it, and then picked it up. Obey came over to get it. I held the umbrella over both of us. He was out of the rain at last.

"It's too wet to play, Obe. C'mon with me. I got to return

122

this umbrella to Pa. He forgot it again. C'mon. Afterward I'm goin' to the library. I got *The Open Man* reserved."

"What's that?"

"Book by Dave DeBuscherre of the Knicks." I took a couple of tentative steps, holding the umbrella high. Obey came with me without thinking. God bless the big bank umbrella. It was keeping the rain off us both.

"Is it any good?"

"I don't know. I haven't read it yet."

I took some more steps, slowly. Obey came with me. He wasn't thinking he was moving.

"Why don't Walt Frazier write a book? He's better than DeBuscherre."

"Maybe he has. Anyway, I don't think any of those guys write their own books. They get other guys to do it."

Obey grinned. "Maybe I'll get you to write a book for me someday, Ezell."

"What about?"

We were walking together now, slowly, but together.

"About us guys. Or maybe when I become a big star in the majors. We'll tell them how I did it."

"How it all started with the Atlas Movers. Your first team. The one you quit on."

"Now cut it out, Ezell."

"You're the one that's cuttin' out, Obey."

"And you're twistin' words."

"Maybe, but I don't want to see us forfeit. And you do."

Obey was silent. We were walking up Fourth now, toward the business district. The umbrella was keeping us both dry. I didn't know how this was going to end, but I knew I had to keep Obey with me. I had to keep in contact with him.

"No, I don't," Obey said. "But what happened last night

123

was bad. Real bad. I'll kill someone next time, so I don't want there to be a next time. You know what I'm talking about, Ezell?"

"Yeah. But maybe there won't be a next time."

"There will be, Ezell. I like your pa in a lot of ways, but he shouldn't be coaching. He won't stand up. He can't. I can even see why, but I don't want to be there when it happens again."

"I don't either," I said.

And that shut Obey up, and it shut me up too. We were about a block away from the bank parking lot. We could both see Pa directing traffic in it. Obey slowed up. I kept on going. The rain kept on coming down. Obey moved along with me under the umbrella. Bless the rain, I thought.

All parking lots are messy when it rains, but the Arborville Bank parking lot is worse than the others because it's not that big and everyone always seems to want to use it at once, especially when it's raining.

When Obey and I arrived at the lot, Pa was directing a Pontiac in and a foreign car out. Both were driven by ladies. There was a lot of horn honking from a Ford that wanted Pa to wave her in before the Pontiac.

"What a mess," Obey said.

"Let's run for it."

I took off and Obey came behind me. We headed for Pa's office which was on an island in the center of the lot. I could hear Pa yelling: "You're all right. Just cut hard to your right. No, ma'am. That's your left. Your right is how you should turn it. There you go—"

Obey and I felt like a couple of football players doing some fancy broken field running around cars, while down the rain came. We made the office OK. I collapsed the umbrella and followed Obey inside. There was hardly room for both of us in there. And no sooner had we got inside than a familiar voice came knifing through the air.

"What're you kids doing in there?"

Obey and I spun around. It was Mr. Gardner himself, sitting in his Cadillac, pulled up to the other window. He was giving us a hard look. He didn't recognize us out of uniform.

Obey swore softly.

"Easy," I said nervously.

"You kids don't belong in there. Beat it."

Neither of us moved. As far as I was concerned, we did too belong there. We were delivering an umbrella.

But when Mr. Gardner saw neither of us was going to obey him, he got out of his car.

"Willie," he called out, "there's some kids in your shack."

Pa looked startled, and then he saw us. "Why, that's my son Ezell, and my captain Obey Parker." Pa came toward us.

Be tough, Pa, I prayed. Please be tough.

"I don't care who it is, Willie. They don't belong there. Get them out." Mr. Gardner reached into his car and took out an umbrella. "Park it for me, Willie," he said, and flipped his car keys through the rain to Pa. Pa caught the keys with his right hand. "I'll be leaving in an hour, so put it nearby," Mr. Gardner added and started off to the parking lot entrance to his bank.

Pa stood there, keys in his hand, the rain coming down on his head. Obey and I watched him, and suddenly we were both scared because we knew he was going to do something.

"Mr. Gardner," Pa called out.

Mr. Gardner turned around.

"Go park your car yourself," Pa said, and he threw the keys right back at Mr. Gardner. Mr. Gardner was so stunned he didn't put up his hand to catch them. They smacked up against his chest and fell to the wet asphalt.

And then he stood there as if he couldn't believe what had just happened. Obey and I held our breath. Then Mr. Gardner bent down and picked up his keys.

Pa came into the office. He looked at me, and then he looked at Obey, and all three of us were squeezed together, and then Pa pushed his wet porkpie back on his head and started to laugh.

"Pa," I said.

"It's OK, Ezell. What's he doing, Obey?"

"He's still standing there, Mr. Corkins. He's got the keys in his hand."

"What're you gonna do, Pa?"

"Nothing. Maybe tell him to park his car 'cause it's blocking the lot."

He's getting into his car."

Pa breathed out a sigh of relief.

"That's good," Pa said.

"The rat is going to park it himself. Way to go, Mr. Corkins."

"Thank you, Obey."

"Gee, Pa, aren't you worried?"

"I don't know," Pa said, and laughed. "I guess I will be."

We watched Mr. Gardner park his own car and then get out, slam his door, and stamp into the bank.

"He's gonna make trouble, Mr. Corkins."

Pa nodded. A horn sounded. Pa looked. He shook his head. "That's old Mrs. Knight. She claims she can't drive into this lot without me helping her. There's the umbrella. Thank you for bringing it down, boys. I was hoping we'd be able to have a late practice today, but I guess this rain washes it all out. So it's Monday night for sure and that'll

126

be one game they can't call because of darkness, ain't that right, Obey?"

Now it was my turn to hold my breath. Be good, Obey, I thought. Be big.

"I guess not," Obey said.

Pa stepped out into the rain and opened up the big umbrella. He winked at us both and started off to help Mrs. Knight maneuver her car into a parking space.

"Hey, Mr. Corkins," Obey said, and he was grinning.

Pa turned.

"That was a great throw," Obey said.

Pa laughed, waved, and went off to help the old lady.

Obey looked at me. "What's gonna happen to your pa now?"

"I don't know."

"He showed a lot of guts."

"Didn't he?" I said proudly.

Obey slapped me on the back. "C'mon, man, let's go to bookville."

"You gonna play Monday night?"

"You're darn tootin' I'm gonna play. That man may fire your pa from his job, but he's all washed up givin' orders. Right?"

"Right," I said.

And we took off for the library, running and yelling through the rain. I didn't feel a drop.

FIFTEEN

WE STAYED LONGER at the library than I figured, mostly because it started thundering and lightning. When it let up we went home. I lent Obey the basketball book and I got out a book about hockey. I don't play hockey, but I like to read about it.

When I got home, Ma asked me if I'd delivered the umbrella OK, and I said "Yeah." I wondered if I should tell her about what happened, but I decided not to. If Pa was fired, he'd want to tell her himself.

It rained all that afternoon and I waited on pins and needles for Pa to get home. I tried reading the hockey book to take my mind off whether he was fired for throwing Mr. Gardner's car keys back at him, but the hockey book wasn't any good, it was all about some kid who was sorry he wasn't born a Canadian and the reader was supposed to feel sorry for him too. Nuts to him. I put the book down and looked out the window. No Pa.

I teased the twins for a while and then tried to check out of that. But it's a lot easier to start a game with kids than to finish one.

Finally I heard Pa's steps outside, and I listened hard. I'd know if he was fired by how he hit those front steps. He came up either slow or happy. I don't mean he took the steps two at a time. He never did that, but he would either clomp down full foot, which meant he was tired and sad, or he'd come down toe first and quick which meant he was feeling peppy.

Pa came down toe first.

I ran to the door, but the twins beat me to him. They usually do. They wanted cookies. On Fridays the bank serves cookies to people waiting to take out new savings accounts. If there's a lot left over, Pa sometimes brings some home.

"No cookies today," Pa said.

"Why not?" Louisa demanded.

" 'Cause I didn't have time to get any. Where's your mother, Ezell?"

"In the kitchen, Mr. Corkins," Ma answered. "Where else?"

"Well, I got some news for you, and for you too, Ezell."

Pa didn't even take off his raincoat. He marched right into the kitchen, dripping a little from his porkpie as well as his coat.

"This was a clean floor, Mr. Corkins."

"Then let a man dirty it up a little," Pa said, beaming.

"My, you are free with my housework," Ma said, but she wasn't angry. She was pleased to see Pa coming home so happy. I wondered what on earth had happened.

"Ezell, did you tell your mother what happened?"

"Where?"

Pa looked crestfallen. "In the parking lot, that's where."

I shook my head.

Pa grinned. "Bet you thought your old man would get fired, isn't that right?"

I nodded. Pa laughed. Ma looked annoyed. "Just what is going on?"

"Went on, woman. Went."

"All right, Mr. Mysterious Willard Corkins, what went on?"

Pa sat back. "Well, you know how Mr. Robert High and Mighty Gardner always tosses his car keys at me to park his car . . ."

Ma bit her lip. "What did you do, Mr. Corkins?"

"I threw his car keys right back in his face. Didn't I, Ezell?"

"In his chest, Pa."

"It's the same thing," Pa said. "That's what I did. Right back in his face."

"Mr. Corkins, have you gone crazy?"

"No, ma'am, but if you give me a cup of tea I will tell you a most incredible story. Ezell and Obey Parker only saw part of it. What happened later is even better. Sit down, Ezell."

I sat down. The twins started hollering that they were hungry but Ma shushed them out of the kitchen. "Your dinner's coming," she said.

And then while she fixed some tea, Pa told her about the parking lot and how he'd flipped the keys right back at Mr. Gardner. Ma didn't say anything then, and I knew she was caught between approving and being scared. Mr. Gardner was a vice-president of the bank. His father—old man Gardner—was president of the bank. Yet, Pa had hit the steps toe first, Pa was grinning like a happy cat. So we both knew he hadn't been fired . . . yet.

By this time Pa was sipping his tea and Ma and I were both very curious.

"Are you going to tell us, Mr. Corkins, or are you going to drink tea when we should be eating supper?"

"I'll do both, madame," Pa said, giving me a wink, and then he sat back like the lord of the world, which he was in our kitchen, and told us what happened.

About fifteen minutes after Obey and I left the lot and Mr. Gardner had stormed into the bank, they sent Walter Hamilton out to relieve Pa and to tell him to come right away to old man Gardner's office.

"I was a little worried at the time," Pa said with a big grin, which told us he was plenty worried at the time. "Especially since Walter kept cracking his knuckles like he does and saying: 'Willard, what did you do?' And I kept saying: 'I don't know what it could be about.' Hee, hee. I knew perfectly well what it was about."

Walter Hamilton was the bank handyman, he did electrical repairs and carpentry repairs. He was the "inside" man and Pa was the "outside" man, and they covered for each other when vacation time came or if one of them got sick. He took Pa's place in the parking lot.

Pa went into old man Gardner's office.

"Sure enough," Pa continued, "Mr. Robert Gardner was there, sitting in a chair next to the old man's big desk, looking mighty smug and pleased with himself. And there was old man Gardner himself, looking about a hundred years old with those snappy blue eyes. He looked like an old bald eagle.

" 'Sit down, Mr. Corkins,' the old man says to me, and I sit down in a chair near Mr. Robert Gardner. For a minute the old man doesn't say anything. He don't have to. His sidekick up in the skies is doing the talking for him. It is thundering and lightning outside."

"Mr. Corkins," Ma said crossly, "you have set the scene. It is thundering and lightning. We heard the thunder and lightning too, but we did not hear what old man Gardner said to you, so could you please tell your story a little faster?"

The twins were making all kinds of hungry noises in the living room. But I didn't think Pa would be rushed. Some strange and marvelous thing had happened, and Pa was obviously going to take his time telling us about it.

"Woman," Pa said, "have some patience."

"I have the patience, Mr. Corkins. I do not have the time."

Pa ignored her and continued: "Finally, when the thunder stops, the old man says to me: 'Mr. Corkins, do you like working for the Arborville Bank?'

" 'Yes, sir,' I say.

" 'Would you please tell me what your duties consist of, Mr. Corkins?'

" 'Yes, sir. I am in charge of your . . . the bank parking lot. I help the people park their cars and when it is raining I escort them under the bank umbrella to and from the bank, when I can.'

" 'When you can, Mr. Corkins?'

" 'Yes, sir. Sometimes there's just too many at once; some of them gets wet.'

"The old man nods, like he should have thought of that himself. Then he leans forward, like a hanging judge. 'Is it customary for you, Mr. Corkins, to let your son and his friends use your office as a play area?'

"That was the line Mr. Robert Gardner had fed him. I was mad, OK, but I tried not to show it. 'No sir,' I said, 'Ezell and Obey were just delivering the bank umbrella to me.'

132

"Without knowing it, I'd jumped from the frying pan into the fire.

" 'I see,' the old man says, 'and just where had the bank umbrella been?' "

"Oh, Mr. Corkins," Ma interrupted, "I told you your forgetfulness would get us all in trouble. What did you say?"

"I told him the truth. I told him I'd brought it home by mistake. Well, I thought he'd eat me up alive. Yes, sir, that old man's jaw fell open and his eyes snapped and I thought I was a goner. 'A double-sized umbrella,' he says, 'a double-sized umbrella belonging to the Arborville Bank, with the words ARBORVILLE BANK printed on it, and you brought it home by *mistake.*'

" 'Yes, sir. I am forgetful by nature. It rained the other day and I just forgot and walked home under it.'

" 'Mr. Corkins, what else have you forgot that belongs to this bank and walked home with?'

" 'Nothing, sir.' I started to get mad again. Now he was accusing me of being a thief. 'I've never taken anything, anything, that I didn't bring back, because I hadn't meant to take it in the first place. I just hadn't put it back. I—'

" 'Calm down, Mr. Corkins,' he says softly, 'I am not accusing you of taking anything. I am telling you that forgetfulness in a man running a busy parking operation is not a desirable quality. Or don't you think so?'

" 'Yes, sir. I think so.'

" 'All right, now we will proceed to incident number two. An incident that I still find hard to believe, Mr. Corkins. My son tells me that you heaved a set of car keys at him. I told my son that I had known you for years and could not conceive of you doing anything like that. Did you, Mr. Corkins?'

133

Ma and I looked at Pa. He had a very superior look on his face.

"Well, Mr. Corkins," Ma asked, "are you going to tell us what you told old man Gardner, or are you going to sit there looking like God? I have to get supper for the twins."

Pa held up his hand. "Woman, I told old man Gardner just what happened. 'Mr. Gardner,' I said, 'I threw those car keys at Mr. Gardner here, but it's 'cause he threw them first at me. I was returning them just the way I got them!'

"Old man Gardner didn't say a thing. He looked at me, and then he looked at his son. Outside the door I could hear the customers talking low as they waited on lines. The thunder made everything seem quiet.

"The old man kept looking at his son, and finally Mr. Robert Gardner had to speak up. He says, 'Willie's always parked my car. Sometimes I forget to leave the keys in the car, so I toss them to him. That's all I did today. I just tossed the keys at Willie. I do it all the time . . .' He finished a little uneasy 'cause his old man just stared at him.

"And when he finished, the old man snaps: 'All the time?' and Mr. Robert Gardner turns red. He's been caught lying already. Sometimes he forgets to leave the keys in the car . . . bull!

"Then the old man surprised us both. He leans forward. 'And just who is Willie?'

"The question hangs there in midair. Mr. Robert Gardner blinks. 'Who's Willie?' he repeats, like he doesn't get it. 'Why, Willie Corkins, sitting right here.'

" 'Do you mean *Mister* Corkins, Robert?'

"And now Mr. Robert Gardner is beet red. He nods. 'Yes, sir,' he says.

" 'Then call him Mister Corkins.' The old man's voice is like ice. I figure then I'm off the griddle and Mr. Robert

134

Gardner's on it. But I figure wrong. It turns out we're both on it.

"The old man turns to me with those cold blue eyes. 'Mr. Corkins, is it your job to park bank customers' cars for them?'

" 'No, sir.' And now I am starting to worry because I can remember when I first took the job old man Gardner telling me *not* to park anyone's car for them.

" 'Do you park customers' cars, Mr. Corkins?'

" 'Sometimes, sir.'

" 'What times, Mr. Corkins?'

" 'When it's a panicky old lady, sir.'

" 'Is my son a panicky old lady, Mr. Corkins?'

" 'No, sir.'

" 'Is he a customer?'

" 'No, sir.'

" 'But he is a vice-president of this bank, is he not?' "

" 'Yes, sir.'

" 'There are four other vice-presidents of the Arborville Bank, Mr. Corkins. Do you also park their cars for them?'

" 'No, sir.'

" 'I am the president of the Arborville Bank. Have you ever parked my car for me?'

" 'No, sir.'

" 'Then why on God's green earth have you been parking my son's car for him?'

" ' 'Cause he told me to.'

" 'I see,' the old man says, 'and if Mr. Robert Gardner told you to get up on top of our building and fix the roof, would you do that, Mr. Corkins?'

" 'No, sir.'

" 'Because fixing the roof is not part of your job, is it?'

" 'No, sir.'

135

" 'Yet we agreed, you and I, when you first took over the parking lot, that it was *not* your job to park anybody's car for them. Or have you forgot that along with the bank umbrella?'

" 'No, sir.'

" 'Do you know why it's not part of your job, Mr. Corkins?'

" 'No, sir.'

" 'I will tell you why, Mr. Corkins. You are not covered for insurance, should you damage someone else's car. If you damage a panicky old lady's car, if you damage Mr. Robert Gardner's car, or anyone else's car, the Arborville Bank would be liable to a large lawsuit. You are *not* insured as a chauffeur for this bank. Is that clear?'

" 'Yes, sir.'

" 'If I ever see or hear that you have been parking anyone's car again, whether it is my son's car or a panicky old lady's car or anyone under the sun's car, I will consider that just cause for termination of your employment. Is that clear, Mr. Corkins?'

" 'Yes, sir. That is very clear.'

" 'As for the bank umbrella, Mr. Corkins. You will stop being absent-minded and see that it stays here. Is that clear?'

" 'Yes, sir.'

" 'Apart from these two incidents, Mr. Corkins,' the old man says, 'your work here has been entirely satisfactory. I think all our business is now concluded. Unless you have something more you wish to say—'

" 'No, sir. Nothin'.'

" 'Very good. That will be all then, Mr. Corkins.' "

Pa laughed. "I ducked out of there OK, went back outside and told Walter to stop cracking his knuckles, I was

gonna be all right. The old man came out at 4:30 like he always does, walked by me without saying a word, like he always does, got into his old Plymouth and drove off . . . real
slow. A real banker. Then Mr. Robert Gardner comes by.
And he don't look at me, and he don't talk to me, but I can
see he's still hot under the collar, and later I hear from one
of the secretaries that the old man gave him the works. Yes,
ma'am, the works. And that's the end of my story."

"Hmmmm," Ma said.

"What do you mean, 'hmmm'?" Pa asked.

"It is a beautiful story except for its end. Its end isn't so
good."

"Now, woman, what do you mean by that?"

"The end leaves you right where the beginning found
you—in the parking lot. Plus one more thing: you have
made an enemy for life in Mr. Robert Gardner. Some day
he is going to inherit that bank. He will be president. And
then where will you be, Mr. Corkins?"

Pa didn't say anything. He hadn't thought that far
ahead. He looked at Ma finally and said: "You think I
should have backed down? I should have parked his car for
him? Do you think that?"

Ma smiled gently. "No, Mr. Corkins, you did the right
thing. I am really quite proud of you." She brushed a speck
of dirt off his raincoat. "You did very well. Here, let me take
your coat and hang it up."

It was something she rarely did for Pa. She helped him
off with his raincoat, folded it over her arm, and was about
to take it to the front closet.

"What's this?" she asked. She took a screwdriver out of
the pocket. "Mr. Corkins," she said.

Pa looked embarrassed.

"And there's more yet," Ma said. She removed some

137

other things from the pocket. "And what, may I ask, are these things?"

Pa looked unhappy all right. "Fuses," he said, in a small voice. "Spare fuses for the bank. I was supposed to give them to Walter."

"Mr. Corkins, when are you ever going to learn? Old man Gardner bawled you out about this very thing today, and right afterward you do the same thing. He could arrest you for stealing."

"I wouldn't steal his fuses, woman," Pa said, getting angry. "They're heavy-duty fuses. I couldn't use them in this house. I just plain forgot. I don't forget on purpose. I just forget."

"I give up," Ma said.

"They won't need them over the weekend anyways," Pa said. "I'll put them back on Monday."

"Pa," I said, "don't forget we got a game on Monday."

"What game?" Pa asked, with a perfectly straight face.

At that, even Ma broke down and laughed. I laughed too, and so did Pa. It was a happy end to a long day. The only ones who weren't happy were the twins. They still wanted supper and said so, loudly!

SIXTEEN

AFTER SUPPER I went over to Obey's to tell him Pa hadn't been fired. Obey was reading *The Open Man*, and when I asked him how he liked it, he said he wasn't learning anything.

"What did you expect to learn?"

"Somethin' that would've helped me with basketball."

"It's not that kind of book."

Obey threw the book on his bed. "Shoot, there ain't no kind of book can teach you about a sport. Only playin' something teaches you. The only good thing about readin' is, it gets my mother off my back."

"You tell Tom yet?"

"About what?"

"That you're gonna play Monday night."

"Naw. I don't have to tell him something like that."

"Why not?"

" 'Cause he figured all along I was gonna play. He figures no guy in his right mind gives up a chance to play under the lights."

"*Were* you gonna play all along?"

"Who knows? Anyways, playin' under the lights can shorten your baseball career by two years."

"Who told you that?"

Obey grinned. "I read it somewhere."

He was giving me back my own medicine. I picked up a pillow from his bed and threw it at him. He caught it and winged it back and then we were on each other. It wasn't more than five seconds before he spun me around and knocked me down. We were going at it hot and heavy when the door opened and Mrs. Parker stood there, out of breath. She'd sprinted up the stairs, and she wasn't young anymore.

"What . . . is . . . going on . . . here?"

"Ezell started it," Obey said. "I was tryin' to read my book, you know, and Ezell come by and started wrestling me."

Mrs. Parker gave Obey the fishy eye but she knew then it was OK. "Ezell, that was very nice of you to take Obadiah to the library. I hope you two can go regularly now."

"Oh, nuts," Obey said, and lay back on his bed.

It was a good time to make my escape . . . and I did.

The next morning it rained a little, washing out any chance we had to go over to West Park and have a kind of informal batting practice. But the drizzle didn't prevent us from meeting at the playground, playing basketball, and talking over the coming second game with the bank.

Nobody talked about the bank kids, about Robby Gardner; we talked about the lights. Tidwell was worried about the lights. He kept insisting you could get blinded by the lights.

"Bull," Ed Moore said. "Those lights aren't nearly as bright as the sun."

"They're brighter," Tidwell said. The less he knew, the more certain he was in his opinions.

"How can they be brighter?" Claude asked. "Les, the sun is lighting up the whole earth. Those lights are just lighting up Veterans Park. And not all the park either. Just one diamond at a time."

"That's what I mean," Tidwell said. "That's it, Claude. They're aiming those lights right at us."

Tom laughed. "You mean *you*, man. They ain't gonna aim those lights at me. Hey, good shot, Obey."

Obey had just canned a left-handed hook shot. He was practicing shooting with his left hand.

"That phony," Chico muttered.

"Obey?"

"Yeah. Threatening he wouldn't play. He wouldn't give up a chance to play under the lights for anything."

"Those lights are bad news," Tidwell went on. He was talking to himself now.

"How come Obey changed his mind, Ezell?" Claude asked me.

"I don't know. Why ask me?"

"He said to ask you. He said you knew."

"Yeah, what happened, man?"

I shrugged. "My pa told off Mr. Gardner in the bank. Obey and I were there."

"No kidding?"

"Jeez."

"What'd he say?"

"Let's hear it."

I didn't want to tell it but they insisted, so I told about what Pa had done in the parking lot, and they listened like it was the story of David and Goliath, which in a way I guess it was. Chico whistled.

141

"And he didn't get fired?"

"Not yet."

"Your old man showed a lot of class," Ed Moore said.

"Crazy if you ask me," Chico said. "It ain't worth it. No baseball game is."

Claude looked at Chico with contempt. "He didn't do it for baseball, jerk."

"What'd he do it for then?"

"Himself."

Chico thought about it and so did the other guys.

"What'll happen if Mr. Gardner starts taking over again Monday night?"

"Pa won't let him," I said.

"How do you know?"

"I just know."

Tom stood up and rubbed his hands. "It won't make any difference this time. We're gonna beat those guys bad this time. I been waiting all my life to play under the lights and I'm not gonna lose."

"Suppose you can't see," Tidwell said. "Should you wear sunglasses?"

That broke everyone up. Only Tidwell would suggest wearing sunglasses at night.

"Well, you may be scared of the lights, Les," Claude said, "but one thing for sure, they won't let a game be called early 'cause of darkness."

"If those guys come out cocky," Chico said, "I'm gonna belt one again."

"And get thrown out of the league?" Claude said. "We're lucky they didn't bust us right then and there."

"Look out!"

A basketball came flying at us. We all ducked. It had

been thrown hard at us. Obey stood there grinning. "You guys ball players or is this a TV talk show?"

"You could kill someone with a basketball, Parker," Chico said. "I'm glad of one thing, that you ain't our coach anymore."

The guys laughed, but what Chico said meant a lot to me. It meant they all knew Pa was our coach now, for better or for worse.

I hoped that Monday night it would be for the better. I did more than that. Sunday night I prayed. It's a pretty poor thing not to pray to God regularly and then suddenly hit Him with a lot of prayers for your pa and your team, but that's what I did. And crossed my fingers too.

Monday morning was beautiful. Sunny and warm. Pa was cheerful. Before he went off to work, he told me to get a nap that afternoon. "Your rested ball player is your best ball player," he said, and I knew it was something he'd heard or read. But it didn't bother me.

"You decided who you're gonna start, Pa?"

"Tom Martin. Only don't tell him, 'cause he's a worrier and I don't want him worrying. I'm gonna start him and pitch him till the fifth and then let Gary mop up."

Pa talked about it as though it were all settled.

Ma told him to behave himself at the bank and not get into any more hassles with Mr. Gardner and also to put those fuses and the screwdriver back before old man Gardner discovered he'd taken something else home by mistake, and not to forget to take his Thermos, and—

"Fuses?" Pa said, and then he remembered. "I'm glad you reminded me. I clean forgot." And he went off searching through pants pockets for the fuses. Pa was too much.

I stayed around the house all morning helping Ma and then went over to the playground. Tidwell and Gary were there going one on one. Tidwell looked awful. He said he hadn't slept at all the night before. Fly balls kept falling on his head out of the lights. "Like the lights were ball machines," Tidwell said.

Gary laughed. "Don't you worry, Lester," he said, "old Gary is gonna fog 'em through there. Nobody'll hit anything anywhere."

I didn't have the courage to tell Gary he wasn't starting. And I wondered if Pa was going to have trouble with Obey right from the start when he announced that Tom was his starting pitcher.

I tried to put it out of my mind. You can lose a game ahead of time by worrying it too much. I went one on one with Gary and worked hard and gradually forgot about tonight's game.

And then after supper, off we went to the game. Pa, me, Ma, the twins, and Chico and Gary, all in our car. The old Buick felt lower to the ground than ever before. We drove up Miller Avenue and then turned left on Maple and there was the sky lighted up, with lights shining on all the diamonds at Veterans Park. The softball diamonds, the baseball diamonds.

Chico was awed. "It's kind of scary."

Gary whistled softly. He could see himself fogging pitch after pitch through the cool night air.

Pa was grinning.

We turned into the parking lot. There were lots of cars there. Lots of people in Arborville come out weekday nights to watch night ball games at Veterans Park. There are two baseball diamonds and two softball diamonds, so they got a real choice. All the diamonds have lights, scoreboards, stands. Everything felt different here from the regular city parks. It looked—well, professional. The grass looked extra green. The balls and uniforms looked extra white. And I was getting extra butterflies in my stomach.

Pa, on the other hand, looked calm. Like this evening was what he was looking forward to all his life and he knew just how it was going to turn out. Which he couldn't possibly have known. No one could possibly have predicted what happened that night in our revenge game against the bank.

SEVENTEEN

THE INCREDIBLE didn't happen right away. It took its time. It let us get set up for a big victory. It let us think we had the world by the tail, which we did for three and a half innings.

For three and a half innings, the world was ours. We could do no wrong, and the bank team, tight and nervous, could do no right. Mr. Gardner decided to start his son Robby, who had only two innings of eligibility. He wanted to get a quick jump on us. The way it turned out, we jumped on him. Second time around, the curve ball just wasn't the problem it was in last Thursday's game.

Chico beat out a grounder to short. Claude laid down a bunt; Robby Gardner fielded it and foolishly tried to get Chico at second. Chico beat the throw and we had two men on. Mr. Gardner came onto the field and palavered with his son, while we yelled that there was no point in stalling tonight—how little we knew at that moment—and the umps wondered why we were so sarcastic and all, because they were not the same umps who'd worked Thursday's game. Pa knew and Mr. Parker and Mr. Moore, who'd come to the game, knew, but they didn't try to stop us.

Finally Robby Gardner pitched to Obey. He tried to sneak the fast ball over on the inside corner, which is a pretty tough thing to do to a guy like Obey who has got quick wrists and doesn't crowd the plate. Obey's bat flashed around and there was a solid crack and that ball was long gone into left field. Their left fielder turned and ran. He didn't even stick up a glove. He just put his head down and chased the ball, trying to catch up to it before it hit the fence way in deep left. When he caught up with it, Obey was rounding third and charging home like grim death. Their catcher gave him a wide berth, and we jumped Obey as he crossed the plate.

That was all for Robby Gardner. His father took him out and brought in Norm Burns. Burns didn't last much longer. George Copp greeted him with a sharp single to left, Tom bunted a ball, and Burns threw it in the dirt at first. George went to third and Tom to second. Then Ed Moore laid down another bunt and Norm Burns slid on his behind trying to field it. George scored, Tom went to third. Gary then hit a pop-up behind second base that their second baseman dropped. Tom scored and Ed went to third. And that was all for Norm Burns. Mr. Gardner brought in their center fielder. I bunted his first pitch. The center fielder just stood and looked at it. The catcher couldn't move out because Ed was coming in. The third baseman was covering his bag because Gary was rounding second, and the pitcher who was a center fielder just stared distastefully at the ball. I had a single.

And that was how it went. Seven runs before we finally went out. Seven runs against the bank team. It was the world turned upside down. The champs had become the chumps and the chumps were becoming the champs. Or so I thought.

And thought for three more innings, because Tom pitched well. At first Gary was hurt that he wasn't starting, but when Pa pointed out to him he wanted him to "mop up" and put the "crusher" on, Gary was pleased. Obey thought Pa should start Gary, but Pa said he thought the bank kids would be nervous after last week's game. "They feel guilty about it," Pa said, "and besides, you boys pounded their butts for them. So they're scared a little. Plus, they ain't played under lights either. So let's let them look at a pitcher they ain't seen before."

Pa turned out to be right. Robby Gardner's curve ball wasn't as hard the second time around, but Tom was a whole new ball game to them. And while he wasn't as fast as Gary, he had good control, and having him in the pitcher's box was like having an extra infielder. He was all arms out there, like a spider, he could grab things.

They hit Tom, but we grabbed everything they hit, and the most important play in the field was the first one, because their number one hitter swinging late hit a high fly out to Tidwell in right.

I was scared for Tidwell. Obey was scared. We were all scared.

"All yours, Les," Obey called out, trying to sound calm because before the game Tidwell had kept worrying about the lights and saying he couldn't see and he should have brought sunglasses, and generally driving us crazy, but Les pounded his glove under that high fly and squeezed it into his glove and jumped and yelled: "Hey, it's easy. It's easy."

The fans laughed, and so did we. And that set the tone. The lights were easy and they shone down on our guys making pretty plays in the field. Chico, looking like a pint-sized major leaguer, going into the hole in deep short; Ed Moore barehanding a bunt and whipping it across the dia-

mond; Tom spearing a line drive high in the air; George
Copp catching a pop fly in short right, George who never
moved very hard for anything.

We sang in the field, like we were born to play under
lights, with a scoreboard and a crowd, and some fans of our
own—Mr. Parker yelling out good things to us, and Mr.
Moore clapping his hands, and Pa keeping up his score
sheet, letting Obey coach at third, saying, "Let 'em hit and
run, Mr. Parker. Let 'em have fun."

For three and a half innings, we could do no wrong. In
fact, we never did any wrong really. In the top of the fourth,
we got two more runs when Obey hit his second home run
of the game, a line shot down the right field foul line. They
were pulled way over on him because of his pulling the ball
in the first inning, so he shifted his feet just a little, and they
didn't see it, and he hit the ball into right field. Chico was
on base. The score was 9-2 now. We had it wrapped up. Not
a peep out of the bank team when they came up for their
licks in the bottom of the fourth.

But we were peeping.

"Hey, when're you guys gonna put on the big stall?"

"You prayin' for rain, Bankers?"

"Gonna be an official game soon, punks."

We reminded them of Thursday night in no uncertain
terms. They didn't answer. All the fight had gone out of
them. Pa hadn't said a word to Mr. Gardner, and he hadn't
said a word to Pa. They hadn't shaken hands at the pre-
game ground rules meeting.

The bottom of the fourth started out no differently than
any other inning for them. Their first guy hit a pop fly into
left. Chico went back, but I called him off and took it and
flipped it to Chico who said: "Way to go, baby."

And they whipped it around the infield—which was a

149

mistake, considering the incredible thing that was going to happen in about two minutes.

Their next guy worked Tom to a three and two count, and then he lifted a fly into center field. Gary drifted right, then left, shouted "I got it" when there was no one within thirty feet of him, caught it, and fired a strike to Claude at second. Claude yelled "Ouch," and added: "Way to fire, Gary."

We laughed, and the guys zipped the ball around, using up time because there was all the time in the world to use up. We wanted this game to last forever. It was beautiful.

And then their third man came up—someone from the bottom of the order.

"Last chance to stall, Bankerheads," Chico yelled.

"Stick it in his ear, big Tom."

Tom threw just three pitches. A ball, a strike, and then a second strike. And it was just as he caught the ball back from Obey that the incredible happened, what could not possibly have been predicted happened.

At first I didn't even know it was happening, I was so busy concentrating on the batter. It was only when Tidwell yelled: "Hey, what's going on?" that I realized something strange *was* going on.

The whole right side of the diamond—first base, second base, right field, and right center—was becoming dark. I looked up. The two banks of lights on the right side of the diamond were fading out. Just like that. Out of a clear and starry sky, with not a storm cloud around, the electric lights were going out.

In a moment, half the diamond was in darkness. I couldn't believe it. It was the kind of thing that happened to other people, not to you, that happened in high school football games but not to kids like us. All I could think was

150

lightning wasn't supposed to strike twice in the same place but here it was, striking us twice. God just didn't want us ever to beat the bank team.

"Time out," the ump said, and with that all hell broke loose.

EIGHTEEN

I HAVEN'T used many big words in this story 'cause I don't know many big words, but I've been saving a dandy one for the end. I didn't know the word when the lights went out but the next day when my ma was talking about how we acted when the lights went out, she said we were "paranoiac."

"What's that mean?"

"It means you were crazy. It means you think everyone is out to get you. It means you thought someone actually went and cut a switch so the lights would go out."

To tell the truth, we did think it. You would, too, if lightning was gonna hit you twice in the same place. You'd think someone whose team was losing, someone who wanted the game to be called off, played another time, someone whose team hadn't lost in two years, someone like Mr. Gardner, had got a buddy to turn off the lights. When those lights went out, we went crazy.

Obey screamed at Tom to pitch the ball anyway.

"You can't play with half the field in darkness," Mr. Gardner yelled.

"Get an electrician," someone in the stands yelled.

"Where?" Ed Moore yelled back.

"You just pitch that ball, Martin," Obey yelled at Tom.

"Time out," the ump said to Obey. "I just called time."

"Get out of the batter's box, Brad," Mr. Gardner yelled at his batter. The bank kid started to back out, but Obey grabbed him in a headlock and held him there.

"Get your hands off him," Mr. Gardner said. "Ump, call the game."

"Let's go home," a bank kid on the bench said, and they started packing their equipment bag. That was too much for Ed Moore. He ran over to their bench and kicked the bat out of a kid's hand and told them not to pack a thing. Someone told him to shut up, and Ed hit the kid. Chico ran over and pulled Ed off the kid and together with George they wrestled Ed to the ground. George sat on top of him.

Meanwhile Obey was still holding the batter in a headlock with one arm and yelling for Tom to pitch to his glove.

Mr. Gardner was trying to pull Obey off the kid, the ump was trying to pull Obey off and get Mr. Gardner out of there, too.

"Stay out of it, Coach," the ump gasped. "I can handle it. Let him go, Parker."

"Not till you say 'Play ball,' " Obey said grimly. "That guy cut the lights and we ain't gonna let him rob us a second time. We're finishing this inning."

"Where's your coach? Where's their coach? Where's the Movers' coach?"

"Willie!" Mr. Gardner shouted.

But Pa was nowhere around.

"Ump, their coach has taken off. You better call the game."

I couldn't believe Pa had taken off, but I couldn't see him around either.

"Maybe it was him who turned off the lights," a bank kid sneered.

That did it for me. My blood raced through my head. "Ezell!" Claude shouted.

"Grab him," George yelled.

But there wasn't anything on earth gonna stop me from belting that kid. I took off after him. He got scared and ran. I ran after him, past Claude, past Tom, past the ump, past George still sitting on Ed Moore . . . and then the only thing that could have stopped me, did.

The lights went on again.

I stopped. We all stopped what we were doing and looked up. The two banks of lights had gone on. The diamond was bright again. We stood there in silence, looking at the lights.

It was Obey who broke the silence.

"Play ball," he yelled, letting go of the bank kid. "Let's go, Tom. C'mon, Movers, hump it. Let's go. Ezell, get moving. Gary, hustle. Tidwell, run. Move, you guys, move!"

We moved, all right. We tore out to our positions because we finally realized what Obey was driving at—those lights could go out again.

"Hold on," Mr. Gardner said, "take some practice swings, Brad."

"What's the count, Ump?"

"One ball, two strikes. Pitcher, do you want to warm up?"

"He's hot," Obey said. "He's ready to go. Let's get a batter in there."

"Batter up," the ump said.

Oh, it was wild all right. Ed Moore, his uniform all dirty from where he'd been lying in the dirt, was on third, pounding his glove, yelling "One more, big Tom. One more, baby."

Claude was singing. "Blow it by him, cousin. Blow it by him."

We were all yelling. That poor bank kid didn't have a chance. He stepped in, looked brave. Tom kicked high and threw a pitch as hard as I'd ever seen him throw it. The bank kid swung, missed, Obey squeezed the ball and jumped high in the air. We yelled and ran in. Now let the bloody lights go out for all we cared.

We pounded Tom on the back, almost as if the game was over, but it wasn't.

"Who's up?" Tidwell yelled.

"Who's got the lineup?"

"Mr. Corkins."

"Where's Mr. Corkins?"

"Ezell, where's your pa?"

"There's Papa!" a high little voice screamed out. Louisa was standing on a chair pointing to right field, to the equipment shelter out there. We all looked. Coming out of the equipment shelter, looking up at the lights, were Pa and Mr. Parker. They started grinning and shaking each other's hand.

And I knew then what had happened. I even knew how it had happened. And Ma knew too. She was sitting there grimly. Oh, was Pa gonna catch it, I thought . . . and laughed.

My story really ends here. The rest of the game was a snap. The lights stayed on. We beat the bank 9-2. Tom pitched a hitless fifth inning, and then Gary did just what Pa said he would; he "mopped up" a demoralized bank team.

When it was all over, we ran for Pa. We would have car-

155

ried him around the field, if we could. Because Pa, of all people, had saved our game.

It was Mr. Parker who told everyone what happened.

"When those lights went out, boys, Mr. Corkins looked at me and we both agreed it probably had something to do with the electric storms we'd had over the weekend. So while you guys were whooping and hollering we went down and opened up the electric box in the shelter. Sure enough, a fuse had blown. And that was when your coach showed what he was made of. He came prepared for any emergency on the ball field—"

"Now, Arthur," Pa said blushing, "you better stop right now." He looked sideways at Ma. She was listening, all right.

"No, sir," said Mr. Parker, chuckling, "Mr. Corkins pulled out of his pocket a screwdriver and two heavy-duty fuses. We unscrewed the panel and he replaced the blown fuse and the lights went on again. Now I'm asking you boys, what kind of coach do you got that carries a screwdriver and heavy-duty fuses around to night games?"

"A great one," Obey said grinning.

"An absent-minded one," my mother snapped.

"Here come the losers," Tidwell said.

The bank kids were coming over to shake hands. This was their first loss in two years and some of them were crying.

"Hey, you guys are gonna lose a lot more, so you better stop crying about it," Tidwell said.

"Shut up, Les," Obey said. Obey was all smiles to the bank kids now. "Nice game," he said to each one, and the kid he'd had in the headlock, he patted the top of his head. "Nice game, fella."

Mr. Gardner came over and stuck out his hand. It killed him to do it, but he did it.

"You got a good team . . . Corkins," he said in a funny voice. Maybe he was going to cry too.

"We do our best," Pa said modestly.

Mr. Gardner swallowed, nodded, and took off. Pa watched him go. He pushed the porkpie hat back on his head and scratched his forehead. "Now that was mighty nice of him to come over and shake my hand like that. His first loss in two years. That's tough to take . . . for anyone."

"It's going to be even tougher to take when he finds out you fixed those lights with fuses from his own bank," Ma said.

Pa looked around to see if anyone had heard that. No one had. They were busy reliving the game and pounding each other's palms and stuff.

"Well," Pa said softly, "I don't expect anyone will ever find that out, will they, Ezell?"

"No, sir," I said, but I knew they would. And I've just told the whole story now.

The reason I've told the story of my pa and Obey and how lightning (or darkness) almost struck twice in the same place is because I want the whole world to know how smart my pa is. He kept his head while we were losing ours and saved our victory for us.

My pa's not an athlete; he's a forgetful little guy with a porkpie hat, and people call him "Willie." He doesn't know anything about coaching, but he's a great coach.

Even Obey says so now, and Obey knows.

ABOUT THE AUTHOR

ALFRED SLOTE lives in Ann Arbor, Michigan, where he is active in Little League activities, playing squash, and writing books for young people. He has taught English at Williams College. His previous Little League books are STRANGER ON THE BALL CLUB, JAKE, and THE BIGGEST VICTORY. Mr. Slote and his wife have three sports-minded children.